UPROOTED

UPROOTED

A. B. BISHOP

Kravitz & Sons
INNOVATORS IN PUBLISHING, MARKETING AND ADVERTISING

Kravitz and Sons LLC
204 E Arlington Blvd. Suite B
Greenville, NC 27858

Published by Kravitz and Sons LLC.

ISBN: 979-8-89639-609-3 (sc)
ISBN: 979-8-89639-608-6 (e)

TABLE OF CONTENTS

CHAPTER 1

Beth was sitting in the back yard shade of the late afternoon in an old Adirondack chair made of wood. There were birds fluttering around the birdfeeders and lots of chirps and 'awks' as the blackbirds moved in and out of the area. There was a slight breeze, just warm enough to make her a bit drowsy as she relaxed after the days chores. The cow had been milked and fed; the chickens were picking up grains from the ground from their food. The dogs and cats were finishing their bowls of food and lapping up water.

"What a beautiful time of day," she remarked to the animals.

Beth and Marie had moved to the house on the farm where their friend, Sam had lived, near Julesburg, Colorado. The farm was near the Wall that now separated the East and West. As the West established government, taxes and reestablished order, the cities started growing again. Many jobs and industries had been reestablished. Their city had become almost overwhelming with people moving in and businesses booming, houses being built and rebuilt. Once again traffic was awful as the streets had yet to be fixed and widened to handle the volume. Both ladies had been raised on farms and yearned for the quieter, simpler life. Marie's work in manufacturing solar panels had become very demanding, but as an owner she could electronically manage her work from any location. Beth loved the outdoors and as a writer and HAM radio operator, preferred a quiet location with animals, good radio reception, and peace from the daily rush and noise of the city. Their life together had taken them down many highways and they decided it was time to simplify and still do the work they each loved. The opportunity for getting away from the city presented itself as Sam was moving to teach in one of the universities.

It was quite a nice place with a house and barn, with room for cows, some chickens, lots of pets, and a huge garden. The river was nearby, so irrigation helped the garden, and the fishing was easily accessed by using the 'cart' that Sam had built to run on the railroad tracks to a 'secret' fishing spot. Of course, the best fishing hole was on the other side of the Wall.

Sam had accommodated the lack of consistent power (prior to getting solar) and had lots of logs for the fireplace, a cistern in the rafters of the barn in case of no power to pump the well, an outhouse available if living off the grid was necessary, and a large root cellar built beside the barn, with two entrances in case the snow was too deep to access in the winter. A rope ran from clothesline to barn, as a guide during blizzards or dust storms. He had been quite creative in preparing for about any weather situation, to take care of his stock, as well as himself. Beth and Marie were thrilled to have such a place to find quiet moments, still working as they chose. Beth had a strong radio tower for her HAM radio communication and internet as needed. The internet was not safe to use as there was much propaganda, and personal information was not safe or secure. Marie drove into Julesburg a couple of times a week to connect with sales staff from the Solar Company she partially owned. Manufacturing solar panels and batteries for storage had become more useful for all the rural areas of the country. The electric grid was still unstable outside of urban areas.

They had planted the garden, as it was mid-May. The root cellar was already full of canned goods as Marie was a whiz with canning fruits and vegetables, and they had had plenty from the last years' crops near their home in the city. They liked to share freely with neighbors and friends. This bounty was also wonderful for holiday gift giving!

This particular week, Beth was staying at the house taking care of the animals and planning a couple of fishing trips to stock up fish in the freezer. Marie and her brother, Trucker had planned to connect and drive up to see family in North Dakota for a couple of days. Trucker had picked Marie up this morning at the nearby, secret opening in the Wall. They were excited to visit family they had not seen for several years.

They would keep in contact with Beth as they traveled near the wall, using the portable HAM radio and antenna her friend Gary had helped her build. The neighbors, Mac and Mae Murray had invited Beth over for Sunday dinner. She was planning to make a pecan pie using her mother's treasured recipe.

Trucker had brought her the pecans from one of his over-the-road transport trips to Houston and they exchanged them for canned goods he and Marie were taking north for family.

It promised to be a good week for everyone, being part of family, with friends, and being content to engage in favorite pastimes, like eating, laughing, remembering, and sharing each other's company.

Beth stared at the afternoon sky thinking about all the changes that recent years had produced to place them in this place in time.

The isolation of the West from the East was still a big problem. The West, however, was doing everything it could to rebuild infrastructure and manufacturing to create their own supplies. They were successfully importing needed items through Mexico and Canada. Educational institutions were thriving and bringing along young people's careers. A medical school had been opened, as more physicians, nurses, and lab, radiology, surgical, dental experts had come West through Canada and Mexico to support the healthcare education, hospitals, and industry. There was still news from the East, but most westerners tried to ignore it as long as there was no aggression shown by the East. The dictatorship seemed to keep tight reigns on information that moved or might benefit the West. Canadian public radio was helpful to know what was going on in other parts of the world. Even access to news channels out of Mexico was becoming more beneficial as English speakers learned Spanish. Westerners were starting to learn and integrate multiple languages throughout. Movement of peoples on both the southern and northern borders was congenial. Trade and transportation between both neighbors was beginning to flourish.

Religion and Politics were still touchy subjects. The same disagreements still existed with guns, ethnicity and color, LGBTQ+. There was no army, but National Guard existed in all states, under the guidance of the governors and a governor's alliance including all states.

Good friends and family did their best to focus elsewhere. One thing that change taught them was that they could no longer assume the same values of freedom. Freedom can become limited, and only be free to the people of power holding the high cards. Are people learning how to compromise? What does that really mean to different people from different backgrounds in different corners of the world?

People in the West were adjusting to change, but it too became an assumed normal. How long would this normal last?

Beth sat and contemplated this flow of information in her head. "What else could happen?" She asked herself. The other side of her brain formulated "that could be a loaded question!".

The sun was fading, and the evening was cooling off. Beth got up, checked that the barn door was closed, and the gates shut, then headed for the back door, followed by a small crew of yawning dog and a couple of ducks. The cats were trying to catch the few fireflies that had come out in the dusk. The cow mooed from the barn, as if saying goodnight.

She looked up at the dusky sky and seeing no clouds in the west, where most storms came from, told the dogs "tomorrow we go fishing! First, I make a pie for Sunday!" They all wagged their tails and followed her into the house.

CHAPTER 2

A loud crackle from the other room woke Beth from a deep sleep. She stared at the clock next to the bed to try to focus her sleepy brain to see what time it was.

"Mayday, Mayday" came the next sound from her HAM radio set in the office down the hall. She threw the covers off and got untangled from the pets that were sleeping on the foot of the bed.

"Lab Lady, come in!" It was Gary, the Vietnam Veteran that had taught her everything he knew about HAM radios. "Mayday, Mayday!"

Beth scrambled into the office and picked up the microphone. "Here Vet. What's up at this hour?"

"My set's been chattering for the last hour. Something bad has happened in the West, maybe one of the big cities." Gary went on to explain that the first messages came from near Los Angeles, then HAM operators came on live, moving from West to East. They lost contact with those farthest West, as if a wave was moving from some direction yet unknown and knocking out radio wave communications.

"As best I can tell, there is a 'wave' of something that appears to be knocking out power in the West moving east rapidly. There was some chatter about a huge explosion and fireball. I cannot get clarification, as I keep losing the HAM's I've heard from. All I know is that it's bad and it's moving this way. Public radio is saying a huge cloud is spreading everywhere, like nothing they can describe." Gary was out of breath.

Beth stared at the set. "So what do you think? Do we treat it like a tornado, or uhm, a huge sandstorm, or snowstorm?"

"I don't know. They are talking about blackouts, as in darkness of the sun, as well as electric power." He sighed.

"Like, go to the cellar for a tornado, but plan as if you are stuck there in a blizzard?" Beth was dumbfounded. Her brain started swirling with plans.

"Wish I could help you Lab Lady, but that's what I know. Keep your radio with you, so if we lose power and it comes back up, we can be in contact. Be safe, sister! Pray for us all!" Gary signed off.

Beth ran back to the bedroom, grabbed clothes and boots and dressed rapidly. She also grabbed her travel case with a few necessities like toothbrush and paste, antibiotic, brush, deodorant. Throwing those and a change of clothes in a plastic bag, she tossed it all into the hallway and looked around the room. "Bedding" was all she said, but grabbed a couple of quilts and stuffed them in another bag, hauling both to the backdoor of the kitchen.

Next she put her HAM radio components into a case, grabbed a long antenna cord, taking them to the pile at the back door. She ran into each room and looked around. "Please Lord, help me take what we need." She grabbed a couple of books and a Bible.

Grabbing the radio case and the bags, she opened the kitchen door and took off running toward the barn and cellar. Glancing up, even in the night sky, she caught what looked like a black cloud boiling all around the horizon to the west and growing larger as she got closer to the cellar door. She opened the cellar and hauled everything in, stuffing it in the corner. Then she went back to the house, grabbed a large sack and stuffed food from the pantry and fridge into that. She remembered utensils. She grabbed the dog and cat food, some food bowls and a gallon jug for milk. She ran back to the cellar.

The cloud was almost overhead.

Beth got the cats and dog into the cellar. The cow and chickens were in the barn, getting a little noisy. She wasn't sure if she could get them in the cellar or open the doors and let them out. "Not safe", she thought and grabbed Betsy's rope and pulled her down the steps.

"Thank God this is a huge cellar." Betsy settled down standing in the corner. The chickens were not so easily gathered. She got most.

The dog and cats were hiding under the cot against the wall, the cow in the corner, the chickens hovering around each other. Beth surveyed this scene.

"What am I missing…?" Then it occurred to her, water! She ran up the step into the barn, grabbed a long rubber garden hose, then connected it to the cistern. Using a valve on the other end of the hose, she opened the cistern connection and ran a little water out before shutting the valve on the hose outflow and drug the hose from cistern to cellar, grabbed a tool box and a bucket, then she closed the cellar door that led from the barn. She then walked up the steps of the cellar door leading outside, once again looked at the menagerie down in the cellar. All the animals eyed her suspiciously.

Listening at the outer cellar door, she noticed that the wind was whistling through the trees now, and as she cracked the door, saw nothing. The air smelled different, like hot, but she could not define it. The sky had become totally pitch dark and she could barely make out the back porch light outside the kitchen door. She shut and latched the cellar door and walked down the steps making sure she didn't step on the chickens, then sat on the cot with the dog. They had one light in the middle of the cellar, with plug-ins. The power was coming from the solar batteries at night, so it should stay on for hours.

They were all breathing and listening as the noise outside got louder. There was a lot of wind, and it was full of a dust-like debris. It sounded like pellets were slamming into the wall of the barn. There was no rain or hail that she could hear. It seemed to get hot and the air smelled funny, like sulfur from a match when you strike it.

"How could a cloud like that come from all around us? What is causing it?" she thought out loud. "It doesn't smell like anything I can recognize." It made her feel funny talking to herself.

She settled onto the cot, the dog and cats huddling against her legs and keeping her warm, so she turned off the light and laid back to try to sleep. She dozed off.

She awoke to a stronger odd smell. It was not from the animals but was acidic and nothing like she had smelled before. It was a mixture of the sulfur smell and maybe smoke. She switched on the light because there was no hint of light in the door cracks. The wind was still howling. Looking at her watch, it was almost eight in the morning. She still had power in the solar battery, for a while. The noise was only the howl of wind and the pelting on the doors. The animals were strangely quiet.

It was time the animals would normally be fed, so she started by putting water in the buckets. After all had their fill, she picked up the poop and put it in a bag near the outer door. Luckily the floor was sand rock. She had shoved a bale of hay and a bag of grain in the door when bringing in the water line, so put some hay and a bit of grain in front of Betsy. The chickens thought that was great and started helping her eat the grain.

Emptying one water bucket into the other, she sat on a stool and milked Betsy. She put a little of the milk out for the cats with some dry food and fed the dogs. She put some of the milk over her own cereal and thought that worked but would prefer her milk cold.

The cellar was warm from the body heat of the close-knit group, and the smell of animals odor was permeating the air like any barn, but it was not too bad. It was mixed with the smoky acidic stench.

With breakfast and early morning chores taken care of, Beth decided she would try to set up the HAM radio and see if there was any communication coming through. The antenna in the barn ran through the cellar along with the power line. She separated it from the power, found a connector that matched the one on her radio set and plugged them together. The radio worked on battery back-up, but she plugged it in to save the battery for later in case it stayed cloudy, and the solar battery ran out.

She started by adjusting the wavelength over the entire range with not so much as a crackle of response. That told her there was not going to be any connections, so she shut it down but left it in a standby mode in case someone tried to get through.

She read a bit until the power started to blink. There was no power being generated due to the darkness. She lit a candle, petted all the animals that were amazingly calm, then sang a few songs she remembered, mostly hymns she knew from childhood.

Every couple of hours she would refill the water pans with a little water, then pick up the poop and manure as needed. The chickens seemed to move constantly. Betsy seemed content to chew her cud. The dogs and cats slept a lot, and Beth dozed off too.

When she woke up, she glanced at her watch to see it was early evening. The winds had died down a bit, and the smell was no longer acrid. Since it was now dark on a normal evening, she could not tell if it had lightened up. She did know that it was a long night ahead of her, as there was little she could assess or do in the dark, with no power.

Beth repeated the same chores she had performed this morning, feeding, cleaning, watering, and offering pats and hugs of comfort to each of the animals. She did find a couple of eggs that the hens had laid. Betsy was glad to be milked, and the cats were thrilled to have some fresh milk, again.

She sat on the edge of the cot and lighting another candle, she prayed. "Whatever tomorrow brings us Lord, keep us safe. I pray that Marie and Trucker are safe. Be with our family and friends during this strange time. Guide us in all things. Thank you for this cellar, with food, water and a place to rest. Amen."

It is hard to know what to pray for, when you do not know what has happened. They slept fitfully through the night.

Chapter 3

Trucker had done most of the driving early in his trip with Marie to try to visit family in North Dakota. They had taken the route north along the old interstate through Wyoming before turning east into South Dakota. The Wall was not an issue to get past when driving through the American Indian Reservation. They did have to be diligent in finding diesel as they moved along the miles, as finding good fuel supply was never assured along this route. Once in farm country, they knew access to fuel would be a bit more consistent. The East needed the farmers and ranchers to supply food, so they were provided access to the fuel needed to produce crops.

They stopped in Pearfish to fill diesel and switch drivers. It was late afternoon. They both stretched and walked around to get their muscles moving after so much sitting. There were no clouds and it was a sunny spring day.

"I'll grab us a couple of sandwiches. What do you want to drink?" Marie picked up her wallet and turned to Trucker for his reply.

He was starring to the west with his mouth wide open. "Do you see that?" He pointed to the horizon. The sun was going behind a huge dark cloud-like bank, which was surrounded by a very wide and dark ring that seemed to be growing larger by the minutes and covering the sky as it moved toward them. They both stared. Several other people came out of the gas station and were staring at the horizon, as well.

The cloud was billowing higher and higher into the sky until the sun was almost shut out. The cloud was black with a red glow around the edges. It had become dusky in a matter of a minute.

"What is it?" Trucker said in a rhetorical way, knowing it was something crazy that was going on. "I don't know, man, but it seems to be coming this way! I'm outta here". The guy jumped into his pickup and spun out.

Marie looked at Trucker. "It's coming this way, where can we go?"

Trucker ran into the station, then back out again. "Come with me!" He grabbed her by the hand and pulled her into the station. "He has a grease pit in the shop they use for tornados." They both ran that way. Trucker stopped at the food isle and grabbed all the drinks and food he could carry. He shoved twenty-dollar bill at the lady behind the counter. "You better come with us, too!"

There were about eight people that ran down the ladder into the grease pit. Trucker dumped the food and drink and ran back up the ladder. "We need a cover", he shouted at the owner. He opened the shop door, then ran out to his truck. Slamming it into reverse, he spun the wheels, then the truck lurched forward into the shop, driving over the pit. Jumping out, he looked around and found a couple of large chains, hauled them to the edge of the pit and yelled "get out of the way". The chains dropped to the floor of the pit.

Running down the ladder, he grabbed the biggest one of the guys and said "we need to attach the axles to the base of the pit. It looks like some sort of tornado."

Marie saw what he was doing and grabbed the owner. "Do you have some tarps or covers. There is so much glass in your windows, we need something to cover up with from the debris."

The owner nodded his head and ran up the ladder, grabbed some folded tarps and threw them down into the pit to Marie. She started opening them up with the help of the young clerk making them so everyone could get under them. "We need to get in the west end, as that is where it is going to slam into us".

Trucker and the big guy, Bill, attached the front and the back axles to the elevator jack. Most everyone had gotten under the tarp and made room for them to get under. The wall of cloud slammed into the building with a roar. Glass shattered everywhere. The air was immediately filled with black sand swirling around. Marie grabbed a pile of what looked like clean towels that were sitting in the corner.

"Cover your face, nose, and mouth!" Marie had to scream to be heard above roar.

All eight people grabbed a towel, and some had to be split into two parts, so everyone had a face cover. Four of the group were holding down the edges to the tarps. The whole garage, as well as the pit was filled with the dust that pelted the tarp. The glass having been broken out allowed the wind to drive the sand through the upper part of the garage. The pit was at least somewhat protected.

The sand filled wind was sandblasting everything in its way. At least the small group of eight was protected from the blasting, but the pull of the wind and the heavy towels to keep out the particulate matter made it very hard to breathe. What they could smell was hot, acidic, and smokey?

It just would not stop. The group traded off holding down the tarp. Bill found some gloves they shared and the rest used parts of the towel to make covering for their hands or other uncovered skin areas.

They shared the food and drink that Trucker had grabbed on his way out. They had to yell to be heard. Somehow, they made a plan of rotation and settled into being in the pit and praying for the torrent to end.

CHAPTER 4

Beth was startled awake by Betsy as she was stomping around in her tight spot. The old cow was no longer patient standing in the cramped cellar. She mooed several times.

Beth sat up in bed and realized that she could see Betsy! There were cracks of light coming from the edges around the doors. She also heard a faint humming. The solar was picking up sunlight and the solar battery was storing energy. She stood up and turned on the light in the cellar ceiling. All the animals began moving around, the dogs sniffing at the doors. The light was faint, but she could tell it was no longer a total black-out.

She patted Betsy and asked her "do we dare open the door and check it out".

The dog barked as if replying to her question so she moved to the cellar door to listen, and see what the air smelled like this morning. There seems nothing extremely different from yesterday, except that light was penetrating through whatever was causing the overcast. It still smelled acrid. The wind was now a heavy breeze and nothing like the blast of the previous night.

Taking a deep breath, she unlatched the door to the outside. She pushed up on the door but it felt heavy and did not want to move. She gave it a shove and felt something move that was on top of it, like maybe a tree limb. She tried again, but it was not budging.

Hoping for better luck, she switched to the door that entered the barn. Knowing that there could have been stuff blowing around in the barn, or damage to the roof, she gave this door a gentle push to see how it would move. It moved a little, so she shoved harder. This time something moved off of the door and allowed her to get it open enough to view the floor of the barn. The dogs and cats scooted out the opening she had created.

The chickens were squawking and milling around the cellar floor. Betsy came up behind Beth. Beth moved her legs up a couple of steps to get them under her to push the door further open. It worked! She opened the door almost fully and held it until she could see what was in the way of latching it open. Betsy followed her up the steps and almost pushed Beth over as she came out of the cellar, all the chickens at her heels.

It was clear to Beth by looking around that the barn had taken a beating. There was a hay bale that had landed on the cellar door and the whole stack of bales had been pushed over by the torrent. Some were still up against the wall of the barn, and maybe even holding it up. The roof had lots of gaps showing as the metal roofing had been torn off in places. One of the big sliding barn doors was laying flat on the ground; another of the big doors was being held by a single hinge. The machinery and heavy equipment parked in the barn appeared to be intact, but there was lots of brush, debris, and black sandy residue on everything.

Betsy did not seem to care. She headed for her stall in search of food and water. It was feeding and milking time.

Beth was not quite ready to get down to routine chores. She needed to see if the house was still standing. She moved out the opening, watching her step as she went, then stopped as she caught sight of the house. It was still standing! There were lots of tree limbs in the yard, and one of the big old elms near the creek had been torn down with the roots bared. She did see that lots of the roofing was missing and the solar panels had some damage, but thought most should be alright as the solar battery was collecting energy. She knew she had lots to assess, but for now needed to get the chickens, dog, cats, and Betsy the cow fed and taken care of for this moment. She didn't want to have to hunt for the cow later in the day. A small part of her was relieved.

She went to the outer door of the cellar and pulled a huge limb off the door and cleared a pathway out of the cellar from that door. Then she opened that door and secured it, walking down the steps to collect food and buckets. She plugged in the HAM radio, so she could hear if there was any chatter on it. She proceeded to get Betsy in her stall with fresh food and water after cleaning out the troughs. Then she sat down on the milking stool and milked the cow.

Throwing out chicken food and refilling their water, she got the chickens into the chicken coop and found that there were a couple of other chickens that had wandered back in from the wooded area. She had to pick up the wire fence in a couple of places, to try to keep them in, but that was all she could do for this moment.

Beth headed for the back door of the house with the idea that she would feed the dogs and cats. As she passed the well, she heard water gushing, so she ran into the backdoor and shut down power to the well pump. "Guess I have to fix a broken water pipe from the well." She began making a list in her head of the first 'to-do's.

When the dog and cats were fed and watered, Beth went back to the cellar to retrieve her radio and other things belonging in the house. With her arms loaded she came up from the cellar and noticed that the sky was darkening again. There was a heavy haze and the acrid smell was back. A sudden gush of wind almost pushed her backwards into the cellar.

She steadied herself, pausing for only a moment, then ran to the backdoor of the house. The door slammed behind her from the force of the wind. Pulling the curtains over all the windows, in case they broke, she counted dog and cat heads to make sure they were all with her. The cats were hard to find as they were hiding behind the washer and dryer, away from the windows and the noise of the wind. The dog was right on her heels.

She gathered the parts of the HAM radio set and headed for the office where her connections were located. Hooking it up, she then powered it on, as another heavy gust of wind and sand slammed into the house. She started searching for a channel where someone was available to respond. As she turned the dial, she slowed down the turn and waited for any radio noise. After she worked through the entire range, she then started turning in the reverse direction, very slowly. She was hearing nothing on her reciever.

"If this is happening all over, then everyone is probably hunkered down. Do we go back to the cellar or isolate in the house?" She looked at the animals as she talked to herself out loud. They were all wide eyed and very quiet.

She got up and moved the desk and chairs into the hallway, then closed the doors. The hall gave her protection from the windows breaking and the hall provided support walls. This was where she would make her stand, for now. She shut all the doors she could and brought blankets, water and food into the hall for the animals. The hall was open to the kitchen, so she rolled the refrigerator into the opening and turned it where she could also get into it for food.

This time the dark windstorm did not last as long, but it was very dark as if night settled in again.

Beth pulled her chair up to the computer table. She had power at the moment, so she brought up the internet. She would not use this method of communication as it was not secure and full of propaganda, hatred, and fear. She thought she might get a clue of what this wind, acrid smell, and crazy weather was about. In this area, they normally got very little connection. There was a fuzzy picture running, and the person talking seemed frantic, and what they were saying was garbled. Beth strained to hear and understand what was being said.

"All we know is that there has been a volcanic eruption, maybe more than one. The cloud of ash and wind has destroyed most of nearby towns. There have been reports of earthquakes in multiple locations…" and the speaker faded out. All Beth saw on the screen was fuzz.

"Where did it happen," shouted Beth, and she pounded her fist on the table. "What is going on?" She sat down, confused, scared, and alone.

Then she thought of her neighbors, the Murrays.

"I have to find out if they are okay."

Beth wrapped a coat around her and a towel to protect her head and ears. She peering out the door, then braved a first step.

The haze was heavy and the air they breathed seemed full of grit. The acrid smell was still all around them, but the wind was not blowing so hard. Then she looked up, Beth only saw the smoky haze.

Her dog Sami trailed closely behind Beth, not daring to lose sight of her, lest something would happen again. The dog did not want to get separated from her. They walked down the trail toward Murray's with caution, as they had no idea what the next steps might bring. There was no protection and Beth had not even thought about it until they headed down the trail. She needed to connect with someone during this strange unknown event. Her house and barn were no longer in sight. The brush, trees and thicket offered little protection were another heavy burst of wind and dust to hit her. There seemed no predictability.

Beth moved on though, holding her jacket close to her face. She was driven by the need to be with other people and connect to try to understand what had occurred around them. She needed her neighbors to be at the other end of this path.

Suddenly the ground shook and tumbled all around them, throwing Beth and Sami to the ground. She grabbed for the dog and managed to hold on to her and tried to cover Sami's head and her own as tree limbs, brush and debris flew all around them. The shaking stopped after a few minutes, but she could still hear the rumble as it seemed to move away from them. She waited a few minutes, praying for the ground to be still. Then she got up, looking around at the hazy woods. It seemed to sigh as the calm returned. She stroked the dog's ears and made sure her legs were steady before taking a step.

"Walk with me Lord. We are in new territory." Each new step through the darkness got her closer to the Murray farm.

Topping a small rise in the path, she spotted the farm ahead of them just down the hill. They did not have the trees and brush that Beth and Marie's place was surrounded by. The area was more open, and she could see the river in the distance. Because there was less obstruction to her view, the wind damage to Murray's house was apparent. There were broken windows all around and sheets of roofing lay on the ground. The chicken coop next to the barn had been flattened. The sliding barn door had been ripped from its hinges and lay askew across the opening. There was no activity in the yard until their dog darted from the house and started barking at Beth and Sami. Sami took off to greet Pepper, who seemed thrilled to see them.

Mae Murray opened the doors of the porch looking at the point of Pepper's excitement. Spotting, Beth, she waved and started moving toward her with an obvious limp. Beth jogged down the slope to meet her, doing her best to avoid all the debris.

"Oh Beth, I'm so glad to see you are okay," she was sobbing and grabbed Beth and hugged her. "Where's Marie?"

Beth explained quickly that Marie was traveling with her brother and had left the day before all this happened.

"You must have hurt your leg, Mae. Where is Mac?" Beth looked toward the barn.

Mae grabbed Beth's arm and started leading her toward the house. "He's hurt. When the wind started, he was in the barn. It tore the door off and fell on him as he was leading our cow in. I'm not sure but he must have a broken arm and is in a lot of pain. I hurt my knee when I was pulling him out from under the door. It hit our old cow as it fell on them and that probably saved Mac's life."

They walked into the porch and both the dogs followed. Mac was laying on the couch with an ice pack on his shoulder and a cloth made into a sling to hold his arm. He was sipping a small glass of whiskey.

Beth asked where it hurt the most, then felt up and down the bones in the arm to feel if anything was broken. There was swelling inside his left shoulder, so she traced the area of the collar bone. He winced.

Beth could not feel any major break but suspected that the collar bone was broken. Trying to distract Mac, she asked "So how did the other guy come out in this fight?" Mac just grinned.

"I'm worried about Molly. She's an old cow and took a hit from that door," Mac grimaced when he moved to get more comfortable.

"Is John around?" asked Beth. John was their young adult son.

"No," said Mac. "He started college in Fort Collins a couple of weeks ago. We pray he is safe."

Beth paused. "What happened to cause all of this, do you think? The massive winds, the acrid smell, the black out of the sun, earthquakes that keep happening. We seem to have had a couple of events, but nothing like the first 'hit'. I don't even know what to call it."

Mac and Mae both just shook their heads. "It sort of reminds me of the pictures we saw on TV in the 80's when Mount St. Helens erupted in Washington. That was devastating and reduced hundreds of square miles to wasteland. But we don't have any volcanos near us, do we?"

"I don't think there are any in Colorado, but there are a bunch of dormant ones in New Mexico and Arizona. Doesn't Yellowstone National Park have some sort of potential for a volcano?"

"Yes," said Mae. "When we visited there several years ago, we learned about the super volcano that hasn't erupted for thousands of years. Could that even be possible? Surely someone would have known if it was about to pop!"

"If that's the case, it's not done yet, either." Mac sighed.

Mae stood up, needing to do something normal. "Well, while we have some power left, I need to draw some water for us and the animals." She looked at Beth. "Would you mind checking on Molly, maybe seeing if she will let you milk her? Oh, and check for eggs around what is left of the chicken house.

Some might have survived."

"Sure", said Beth. She got up and headed for the barn.

Molly was standing in her stall in the barn but was clearly spooked. She calmed with Beth's attention to her, as she got her water and fresh hay. When she grabbed the milking stool and milk pail, Molly seemed to approve, and Beth milked the old cow. After she was done, she carried the milk pale with her to the hen house, sitting it down on a stump and searched under boards for eggs. She also found a couple of chickens that had been crushed when the building fell. Beth grabbed them in one hand and rolled up her shirt to carry what eggs she could find. Then she grabbed the milk pale in the other hand and carried it all to the house.

Mac had fallen asleep on the couch.

Beth sat down at the kitchen table and started plucking the chickens. Thinking about their discussion, she was speculating about what to do next. The two women began thinking and talking out loud while they worked on making dinner.

"We don't know what it really is or if it is done. We have lots of damage at our place, and so do you.

I'm missing my partner, who is somewhere north of here in one of the Dakotas with her brother. I pray they are okay." Beth paused for a moment, then continued. "With Mac hurt, what do you say we pool our resources. Is your water well running okay?"

"I think so," said Mae. I watered in the barn, and it is running here in the house for now. But it won't work for long, as the power is about gone from the battery. I'll be drawing water manually soon without sun."

"We have power right now at my house as the generator is working. I found a water leak but I should be able to fix it. My HAM radio should operate too, and we might be able to contact someone. It was Vet Gary that first warned me to go to the cellar. I know the generator was working when I left earlier."

"How about we combine resources, take the animals to our place, and you and Mac come stay, for now.

We are going to need each other," Beth suggested.

Mae looked at Beth. "You are right, we need each other. I'll convince Mac when he wakes up."

Beth stood up and handed Mae the plucked chickens. "Okay, I need to get home and repair the water line then milk our cow. I'll be back later if nothing happens to get in our way. We can move the animals. You can drive Mac up to my house in your truck."

The women hugged and Beth called her Sami and hurried up the trail to start repairs.

CHAPTER 5

Marie and Trucker worked to keep everyone calm in the pit. With the sudden rushes of winds and grit, the starting and shaking or rugged earthquakes, with the roll of thunder as they moved away, it was not an easy task. Everyone got tense when the most recent quake cracked the wall on the side of the pit and down across the floor.

"Will it ever stop?" sobbed Grace, the young woman from the store.

Marie reached over and hugged her tight.

"I don't know honey, but we're all still here and unhurt. We can make the best of it", and Marie looked at Trucker with the same question in her eyes.

Trucker turned to Bill. "Maybe we should unhook the axles and get the truck off the pit. Anybody got a big cellar nearby, so we have a place to get away from another round of tornadic sandstorms?"

The station owner stood up. "My wife's a teacher at the high school. I bet the kids are all in the basement over there. I need to check on her and our kids."

A couple of other guys spoke up with "I got kids there too!"

"Okay", and Trucker nodded at Bill. They unhooked the chains and climbed out of the pit. The rest of the group followed cautiously. Everyone helped each other in the climb, and they all pitched in to clear away large limbs and heavy debris from the top of the pickup and the driveway up to the store and station. The street beyond the store looked like a field of debris and trash. The group worked quietly, but showed the bewilderment, fear, amazement and horror they were feeling as they surveyed the surrounding view. Cars were overturned, trees were uprooted. Power lines lay on the ground.

Windows were broken out. A house had been leveled nearby. The water tower that sat high above the town, about a quarter of a mile away, was leaning precariously on its support legs.

There was no sunlight, just the gritty haze and a darkly clouded sky. The wind bursts that rolled through were hot and smelled of burnt wood and were filled with grit that stung their faces as it blew. The ground again began to rumble and shake around them but subsided before anything big happened this time.

Trucker backed the pickup out of the shop, and everyone climbed into the cab or the pickup bed. Bill pointed the way to the street that would take them to the school, but Trucker was having to go slow and weave around obstacles on the pavement. The pavement, too, was cracked and had multiple upheaval areas as they moved along in the direction of the school. As they pulled into the entrance area of the building, Marie and Grace shrieked as they pointed to the water tower as it crashed to the ground, dumping hundreds of gallons of water.

The wind picked up with tornadic force, loaded with the black grit. The pickup arrived at the school parking lot and the group quickly covered nose and mouth and ran toward the building entrance. The door stood open as it had been left to stand that way since the first big blow of the 'storm'. A couple of the group attempted to shut it and pushed up a couple of heavy book cases to hold it shut. Marie stopped them.

"Look," she said and pointed out to the parking lot. Other cars had pulled in and people were climbing out carrying small children, blankets, bags, and other things and running for the door they were trying to close.

"I think the whole town needs a place to gather", and they pulled the bookcases away to let the people enter. Marie led the newcomers toward the nearest staircase that went down toward the basement. A couple of adults were coming up from the basement to see what the new noise was about. They waved at the people and showed them where to go once in the basement area.

Once everyone was inside (at least from this group), the guys again tried to shut the doors and hold them in place with the heavy bookcases. In the basement, they shut those doors to keep out the grit as the winds swirled down the stairs. This gathering place was not yet done allowing other people to enter.

Chapter 6

In the central part of North and Central America, from Yellowstone south beyond Mexico City and north through Canada to the Artic Circle, there were multiple eruptions of newly active volcanos, that had been dormant for thousands of years. The earth shook with earthquakes and huge fault lines had opened up in the earth. When the Yellowstone Caldera erupted, it triggered massive seismic rifts, allowing hot lava to rise from the earth's core.

There had been little warning, as monitors were set off in known areas with an almost synchronous timing over these thousands of miles.

It was like a crack had broken open to the core of the earth and was tearing the American continents into pieces. The earth around the perimeters shook and rumbled. The sky was dark with soot and ash. It was hard for animals and humans to breathe for hundreds of miles on either side. Buildings were toppled, pipelines of gas, water, oil ruptured. The great hot winds raked and burned the land of its trees, vegetation, and man-made structures. Whole cities near the eruptions were destroyed, killing anything within the perimeter of two hundred miles in all directions with ash, lava, and winds flaming burning trees. Miles beyond that, there was no available power, water, sewer, transportation or communication. Bridges and roads were destroyed. Dams were felled by the heavy earthquakes, and what was not burning, was now flooding. Airplanes crashed. The continental power grid was broken.

The people that survived the eruption, the quakes, the fires and flooding sat where they were caught, holding loved ones and thinking of survival. What happened and why? Where is our help? Who will come? Where do we go? How long do we have to wait? How do we survive? Their questions were unanswered. Most area from California to the Mississippi River was cut off from communication and services. Even the large cities of the Eastern coasts sat in the darkness of the sky, with disrupted services. Food and supplies that normally flowed into the great population areas ceased at this time. There was no television or radio to tell people what to do or what to think. Satellite communication was cut off by the heavy ash and soot that blew across the continent, and beyond. The oceans were crazed by sea floor upheaval from Canada to South America. Boats sank.

There had been warnings, for years.

The response had been as insignificant as the survivors felt at this moment.

There had been no significant action to mitigate man's impact on the earth that was home. No preparations were made for this devastation. No answer would be readily forthcoming.

Is this to be the end or the 'new' beginning?

CHAPTER 7

"Thank you, God for this food and for this roof over our head. Be with our loved ones and hold them in the palm of your hand", Mac prayed the blessing as they sat around the fireplace at Beth and Marie's home.

Mae had cooked both the chickens that had been caught in the destruction of the coop. They would eat on this food over the next couple of days. Beth had brought up canned beans and beets from the cellar to compliment the meal.

Finding some pain killers, Mac was feeling better even though his arm was in a sling. Mae's limp had improved with some ointment massaged into the muscles. They all sat companionably around the fireplace and all the dogs and cats were nearby.

"Have you heard anything on your shortwave radio?" asked Mac.

"Not yet, but the skies are going to have to clear a bit for anyone to communicate beyond shouting across the room!" Beth grinned and they all chuckled.

"It reminds me of when I was a kid. We used to go visit our grandma. They just lived on the other side of the river. She cooked on an open fire, even baking pies and bread, just like Mae does sometimes for us. Then we would sit around the fireplace and she and Grandpa would tell us kids stories about settling here. That would have been in the early 1900's. They homesteaded here." Mac was enjoying the memories of forgotten times.

"Well, we may have taken a step back into that time, given the uncertainty of this 'event' or whatever it is or means. I'm just glad you folks are here with me!" Beth got up and hugged them both.

"This talk makes me think I will make a pie. I brought some apples that we had. If you have some flower and sugar, we can throw in an egg and have a great cobbler with those apples. It's better they don't ruin." Mae went out to the kitchen with a lantern, then came back with the ingredients, a large bowl and a cast iron pot.

"I hope you don't mind, I raided your pots and pans, "Mae said. "Help yourself to whatever we have," replied Beth. "Can I help?" Mae shook her head and started making pie dough.

"Any thoughts about what our next steps should be? There aren't many people in this area anymore or we could gather more together in some central place. We are lucky that the South Platte isn't dammed to the west much or we would see more flooding. If we decide to head out of here, it may be hard to cross." Mac sighed.

Beth thought about what he said. "My guess is that from the direction that the heavy winds blew, going west might not be a good idea. It wasn't weather that caused that, maybe more like you were talking about with Mount St. Helens. Could the caldera in Yellowstone have blown its' top? If so, how bad off are cities like Denver or Fort Collins. Cheyenne probably got blasted for sure and Casper is even closer to Yellowstone."

Mae spoke up. "Is there any use crossing the wall and going east. Won't they reject us like normal, especially if they don't have anything left to share?"

"I wish John was here, we could use the help no matter what direction we go," lamented Mac.

"If the sky clears a bit tomorrow, I want to try to pick up something from the radio. It would help if we could find out how bad things are in other places. I really need to know if Marie and Trucker are safe somewhere out there." Beth stood up. "I will start up the generator in the morning so we can draw water for the animals and ourselves. Thanks for bringing your extra gasoline. It will come in handy for a while if we ration how we use it. I'll scan the radio for anyone listening."

Mac sat up. "Could you go see how the river looks tomorrow, in case we need to prepare for flooding down at our place…not that we could do much to stop it. At least we can see what is moving down stream."

Beth nodded and headed for the kitchen to wash up dishes with Mae. The pie smelled yummy, but it would cool until morning. They finished up and all went to bed.

There were a few rumbles through the night as earthquakes continued but seem less pronounced. The house held solidly, and they managed to rest.

The sky lighted a bit at sunrise but was still a smoky haze. Mae was up first and had milked both cows and collected eggs. Beth went to the barn and fed the stock and tried to give them calming strokes or calm talks. The dogs and cats finished their breakfast in rapid fashion. Beth started the generator then ran water into the troughs for all the animals. Then she collected water into buckets and took them into the house.

Beth turned on her radio and scanned channels rapidly for any hint of activity. Nothing was heard yet.

The three of them sat down to eggs and bacon with fresh biscuits Mae had made. "We get pie later," said Mac. "I was dreaming about apple pie with ice cream, yum…" and he trailed off.

"Thanks for breakfast Mae!" said Beth as she stood up and headed back to the radio. This time she slowly worked the dials, and for a couple of seconds, it sounded like something significant in the static. She searched slowly in the area it first occurred. She could not hear it again.

"We really need the sun to help us with some solar power, then you could leave it on," said Mac. "If the generator could store some power, I could listen while you go check out the river."

"Well, I think it does. It may not be much, but if someone does try contact, you could mark the location and I could try to narrow it down when I get back! Good idea!" Beth went out to the generator and checked the battery for level of storage. There was some available.

She set Mac next to the HAM radio in a comfortable chair, then showed him how to read the dial if he heard something as he was scanning. He would write down the dial location and she could check it later.

Grabbing her fishing gear, she headed for the 'cart' with the dogs to use the railroad track to get them to the best fishing spot. She would be able to check the level of the river and see how much it may have risen, if reservoirs had been impacted upstream. The river dumped into Lake McConaughy, and there was a dam on the lake. This was where the North and South Platte Rivers merged, once again in their meandering, then flowed east. She feared that that dam may have broken with extra waters from broken dams upstream.

The 'cart' was a wonderful re-creation that Sam had done with a manual railroad cart. Beth pumped the arms of the cart gradually moving it along toward the wall. The dogs had jumped on and rode in the seat. Beth picked up speed until she began to approach the wall opening, then she pulled the brake to stop, hopped off and removed the camouflage from the opening and pumped through for a few feet to the east side. She jumped off again and recovered the opening, before moving along the tracks farther.

As she approached the river, she could hear it rushing, and slowed down. The tracks ran along side of it, but not too close. She decided she should approach the river on foot in case it had washed out any of the rails. Walking and listening, she could tell it was running high, but when she finally caught sight of it, she stopped and grabbed both the dogs. It was almost up to the tracks where it had normally been a distance of a football field away. There were loads of brush, trash, huge tree limbs. She even saw a car had washed up on the other side.

Trying to see the place where the river ran through the wall, she gawked at a broad open area that the river had created by breaking down the wall. She had never seen a river in Colorado outside of its banks, but this was amazing! They would not be able to cross the river to the south. As high as it was running, there was great probability that all the small bridges were gone upstream.

Beth did not have any idea if she could get near her fishing hole, given the height of the water spread along what used to be dry land, nowhere near the riverbank. She decided to take the cart back closer to the wall and walk to a small pond that was created when the river waters ran high. Maybe it might be quiet enough that fish would bite if she could get near enough.

She loaded the dogs back on the cart and began pumping in the direction toward the wall. She found the trail she had used before to go to the pond and hopped off with gear in hand and trotted down the narrow trail. The dogs bounded behind her, veering left and right to sniff at new smells, but not getting too far away. Beth stopped as foliage thinned out around her. She saw the pond, which now looked more like a lake that became a part of the flooded plain on the side away from her.

"Well, let's see if there are any fish that might bite," she said as she sat on the ground away from the water and started digging for worms. Finding an abundance of night crawlers, she took only ten or twelve, put them in a small pail with dirt, selected a nice juicy one and planted it on her hook.

She also decided to mark the level of the water and grabbed a small branch and marked the edge of the water by standing it in the mud. Then she sat back down on the ground and focused on fishing.

Without notice, she got a bite and hooked a nice trout. Pulling it in and putting it on her stringer she prepared the hook again and tossed it in. This happened quickly and after about eight fish, she thought she better quit as their refrigeration was limited. This would be a feast for the three of them tonight.

Packing up all of her equipment and the fish, she glanced at the place she had planted the branch. Her mouth fell open as she saw that the pond edge had risen almost two feet since she had started, maybe no longer than an hour ago. The river was continuing to rise and fast.

She and the dogs hurried back to the cart. They loaded up quickly. Beth surveyed the area, as she had never paid attention to the slope of the land. It was rather a gentle slope with no defined rise in elevation anywhere near her. This could clearly mean that if the water continued to rise at the rate it was, the flooding could reach the wall in a matter of hours.

She also knew the Murray ranch was closer to the river and lower in elevation than their place. She needed to get back to the house.

Beth and the dogs passed through the camouflaged area of the wall. She did not even bother recovering the opening but was thankful for the incline that the rails took up to their home.

Mae met Beth at the door.

"Mac has found a track of noises on your radio!" She was excited and hugged Beth.

Beth ran into the radio room where Mac was sitting trying to note location of the signals. He grinned when he saw her and backed his chair out of the way for her to start working the dials. She knelt in front of the set and started refining the signals.

"I had Mae start up the generator again for a bit to keep trying to get a voice, once the static started. You should have a little more time, unless you want me to have her start it up again." Mac stood up waiting for her reply.

"Yes, have her restart it and let it run for a little while," Beth got up and grabbed another chair to sit on and worked the radio.

After lots for noise for a few minutes, she gradually located a clear voice. "MayDay" was the word she clearly identified over and over. "MayDay!"

She spoke into her microphone. "This is Lab Lady, who am I speaking to?"

The repeated "MayDay" paused. "This is TigerPaw," and there was a squawk from the set. "Where are you Lab Lady?"

"We are near the wall close to Ogallala, TigerPaw. Where are you?" Beth asked cautiously.

"Friend, you may be in trouble," said TigerPaw. "The South Platte River is overflowing its banks as all dams have broken here in Denver. Chatfield has flooded much of the inner part of the city, just in the last couple of hours. It is headed your way."

"Okay, TigerPaw. Do you know what has happened to create this mess?" Beth asked, not knowing if she wanted to know or not.

"Only word we had was that Yellowstone crater blew, and from there a chain reaction of earthquakes and other unknown volcanos blew. Also, California is now split by the rift of the San Andres Fault. Lots of damage all over, little power, many tall buildings have…", and he trailed off.

"Do you know Vet Gary?" asked Beth about her friend and mentor.

"I do and have heard from him a couple of times. Power is limited", said TigerPaw. "He was okay last I heard this morning".

"Where is it safe to go? Have you heard from any other part of the country?" Beth was struggling to know what the best questions were to ask.

Static rose in the set. Beth waited for a minute and prayed it would clear.

"You still there Lab Lady?" asked TigerPaw. "Go ahead," she said.

"My power is connected to a TV station I work with. I've been able to hear from Texas, Florida, Illinois and New York, so far. Skys are black. Earthquakes have taken out most power. Mexico is in a world of hurt. California is breaking off as the fault line continues to widen and in some areas is filling with seawater. Power is limited all the way to the Atlantic Ocean. They are shooting people that try to move East past the wall. Panic is rampant in all major cities."

Beth was stunned. "How do you know all of this?"

"It is coming off the wire, when we get a connection. We cannot share it as we have no way to be heard. I'm lucky to have connected with you. People are panicking all over in the Mile High City. Where can you go from your location?" TigerPaw wanted to help.

"I know we can't cross the South Platte and go south or directly east. We might be able to go north. West is not safe." Beth was struggling with trying to find answers.

"Get away from the river and most lakes that are fed by the rivers. Flooding is worsening. I don't know if you can find a way to cross over the North Platte River coming out of Montana, but don't go West. I think we lost many of the major towns and cities in Wyoming. I wish I knew where I could go," TigerPaw sighed.

Mac waved to Beth from the open door and mouthed "generator is off" before moving into the room.

"If you get Vet Gary again, tell him we are migrating north. I'll keep trying to connect. Thank you for your help. Prayers that you stay safe," Beth was in tears as she signed off.

Mac and Mae were standing in the door frame hugging each other. "Oh My God," said Mac. "What do we do?"

"I have to check on something", and Beth ran out the door with the dogs following her. She ran down the trail that led to the Murray ranch. It was only a quarter mile and the trail overlooked the farm after running about half way. She jogged to the highest point, then stopped suddenly and stepped to the side of the trail to lean on a tree. Beth was breathing hard through the course air and bent over to try to not breathe in the grit. She eventually stood up and eyed the downward slope in front of her on the trail.

Her line of sight lifted to identify the buildings of the Murray ranch. The haze was still heavy, but her sight adjusted, and she almost collapsed against the tree as her brain registered what she saw.

"Oh, my Lord," she began, then abruptly turned her back on the sight and started jogging back toward her house. The dogs kept up with her.

She ran into the house as soon as she got there and seeing no one in the porch or kitchen, yelled out

"Mac, Mae, where are you?!"

They both came out of the bedroom where they had been resting.

"What's up?" asked Mac as he yawned.

"Water's rising rapidly. We need to get packed up. It's a lot worse than we thought." Mac's furrowed his brow and he asked "what do you mean?"

Beth rubbed her chin, thinking how best to explain. "The river is way beyond flood stage. The railroad tracks are almost covered beyond the wall. I went to check on your house and the water has flooded your barn and reaches to your house." She paused. "I'm sorry", was all she could think to say as Mac sat down in the nearest chair and Mae grabbed his shoulders.

"We need to figure out what direction we can evacuate toward, now. What can we gather to take with us quickly?" Beth's mind was racing, and she made herself calm down. She ran into the radio room and found a map. Dropping it on the table next to Mac, she ran out and started the generator. She heard the radio squawk as it came on, then fell silent.

Mae sat down next to Mac at the kitchen table. Beth followed their lead, then opened the map, which thankfully was topographical. With elevations marked for the surrounding areas, including Lake McConaughey, rivers and the highways, with portions of the railroad, they could identify the direction that flooding was headed.

The earth rumbled suddenly, and the wind began to howl again. What little light they got was again blotted out. The three of them stood in the doorway praying the support beam above it continued to support the house. The waited for the shaking to subside, but instead it shook harder. Mac lifted his arm and pointed out the back door. The barn appeared to dissolve into the earth as it fell. They held on to the door frame, until Beth just slid to the floor and sat as the world trembled.

"Is this how it ends, Lord?" asked Mae.

Mac hunched over and clenched his fists.

The animals laid down and pressed close to Beth on the floor. She wrapped her arm around them all.

CHAPTER 8

"We need to get out of here," Trucker whispered into Marie's ear as he returned to the basement's temporary kitchen.

Marie had been rolling out bread dough before the latest earthquake and tornadic blast slammed into the big brick school. The vibration had forced people to their knees or knocked them off their feet.

Everyone just waited where they landed for this round of violent movement to subside or end.

Trucker and Marie sat on the concrete floor, leaning against the support beam. The hoped it would withstand this added bout of horrific vibration.

What would be possible steps to get out of this chaos? It must be widespread and recurrence was unpredictable, the intensitiy increasing. "Boom!" cracked loudly above them as something in the building gave way.

"Do you think we can get closer to Mom's?" whispered Marie to Trucker.

He shook his head. "I don't know. We have a full tank of gas, but the roads may be severely damaged, and heaven only knows what other obstacles we might run into. It's going to be a crap shoot to find enough diesel to keep driving, if we can get out of here." He paused.

"Is there a problem if we try to leave?" Marie suspected more.

"Talk is that some of the people in this town want to head East. Nobody has a clue what is going on outside of here. Problem is that, as a group, they want to commandeer anyone and anything to make their plan work. For us to go elsewhere, we need to move quietly and soon." He glanced over to a group of women huddled around another support beam.

After a few minutes, Trucker whispered "Be ready. If it stops quaking, we will look for another distraction that will shift people's focus." He looked around the room and said rather loudly, "I wish we had baked the bread first!"

People nodded but kept themselves near supports for the time being as it was.

They lost track of time as there was no light in the basement. The air was hazy and gritty, even below ground. There were a few lamps, but it was still extremely hard to see. The generators had gone off with the latest earthquake. Buckets of water had been hauled into the basement for cleaning and for flushing toilets to try to maintain sanitary conditions. Lots of the buckets had spilled on the floors.

As the shaking slowed a bit, Marie got up and using a mop, steadied herself. Others had also stood and started trying to work in the kitchen area. "Yep, we still want to eat," commented an older man as he got up and walked to the sink where he had been washing pots.

After another hour, the earth seemed to calm a little bit, so the ovens were heating up and some generators had been started, with some lights cutting through the dim room. The dishwasher was standing near the sink as Marie carried dirty pots over to be cleaned. He had his head lifted to the ceiling like he was sniffing the air.

"What is it?" Marie asked.

"Smells like rotten eggs," and he shook his head. "GAS?" she said.

"Yeah, but from above us." He paused. "May have a broken line upstairs." He then headed for the people standing near the staircase.

A group of them ran up the stairs. About five minutes later, a woman came running down the stairs, stopping to cup her mouth and yell "EVACUATE—gas leak. Turn off all lanterns!"

There was a sudden flurry of activity as panic set in. Others began yelling "Evacuate" and "Gas Leak".

Parents grabbed their children and began running up the stairs, in a mass of bodies.

Marie was being carried along with the panicked group. As the group turned the corner of the stairs, a heavy hand grabbed her arm, pulling her to the right but continuing up the steps. She looked over to see who was pulling her and saw Trucker. They fell into step together, then as they got on the ground floor, he pulled her into a closet. The rest of the evacuees headed for the outside door.

Trucker and Marie waited until all the group left the building. They then headed the opposite direction for another exit.

Chapter 9

Beth grabbed sleeping bags, camping gear and gasoline and shoved it in the back of her little trailer hooked up to the jeep. The portable generator was already loaded. Mae and Mac hauled out a large cooler filled with food, then went back for a large jug of water. Mac and Beth grabbed shotguns and shells. They opened all gates so the animals were free, left the barn doors open, and brought out a box of canned food from the cellar.

Wearing jackets, goggles and face masks, they got into the jeep with all dogs and cats and headed west on the local road. Mac continued to study the map, looking for all alternative roads to avoid rivers and streams that would be flooded. This was a journey for survival as flooding was getting nearer as they traveled the road.

The HAM radio portable unit was hooked up and turned on for any possible connection to humanity in this inhumane time. Mac directed her to take Interstate highway out of Julesburg as it seemed the reasonable route to go west then north without too much flooding of rivers; at least until they got near the North Platte River. He was careful not to guide them too far west before heading north.

Mae sobbed as they left Julesburg, quietly letting go of life as they had known it. She prayed silently for their son, John, who might have escaped from the violent blast that possibly destroyed Fort Collins.

Beth was thinking of Marie and prayed she and Trucker had made it to North Dakota. Sami sat on the console between the seats and pressed her head against Beth's leg. Mac's dog was sitting on his lap as he traced their journey on the map, looking for the safest direction.

They were turned west at the highway out of Sterling. This was a two-lane highway, which was torn up in places by cracked earth. There were only a few farms and ranches off the road and widely scattered. There was an occasional vehicle on the side of the road and Beth always stopped to see if someone needed help. No one was in or around either.

"Let's check the gas tank," said Mac at the first truck the checked. If they didn't run out of gas, they left the vehicle for some other reason."

He had a manual pump, and they found a spare gas can. He pumped several gallons, transferring as much as possible to the jeep's gas tank, then placing the gas can with the remainder in the trailer. Then he would raise the hood of the jeep, open the air filter and clean it out as best he could. He thought this was possibly the reason the cars they found had been left.

They reached intersecting crossroads, just as what little light they had begun to fade. Setting up the tent, they brought in gear needed to eat and sleep, all the animals, and zipped it up tight to filter as much of the larger air particles as possible. They tied it to the west side of the jeep in case they got hit with another tornadic blast. Heavy winds were probably the reason many cars they had passed were on their sides in the ditches.

It seemed a mellow night, compared to the last ones they had stayed in the house, but it was still extremely windy, and the air carried so much grit. They used a small lantern and made sandwiches, fed the animals, and sipped water from bottles.

"If we can find a house or barn, maybe we could ask to stay. The wind and grit is brutal. So glad we have been wearing masks and bandanas over our faces. Wish we could do something for the animals." Beth was looking at their group in the tent. "Are you two doing okay?"

Mae and Mac were leaning on each other and were exhausted. "We are missing our son and mourning our loss of home. Never have we thought this might happen to us." Mae buried her face in Mac's shoulder. He held her tight.

Mac looked at Beth. "I've been wondering if it might give us closure if we went on to Fort Collins," he said quietly.

Beth met his eyes and paused. "I understand", and she shook her head. "Does this road going west lead us toward Fort Collins?"

He nodded.

"Then we head that way in the morning." Beth understood as she was also anxious to find Marie and Trucker. At this moment, they were as close to John as they could be, if they continued north.

The next morning was a bit calmer, but still hazy and overcast. They ate some cereal, then fed and watered the dogs and cats. As they packed their gear, there was a slight tremor to the ground. They hoped it was subsiding and not building.

The two-land road was full of major cracks from the earthquakes, and Beth did her best to maneuver the jeeps as safely as possible. The terrain was flat and seemed very grassy, with few trees. They watched the horizon for any other signs of life.

"What's that?" and Mac pointed ahead of them about a mile. There appeared to be a group of cars moving together and come straight toward them.

Mac pulled out his shotgun and loaded it. Beth was looking for a pull off from the highway to offer a defensive position. She looked back at Mac. He was loading the other shotgun.

They spotted a historical marker coming up on the right. Beth pulled off next to it as Mac watched the cars.

Mae read the sign. "This is the location of the Pawnee National Grasslands." She held the dogs to keep them calm, as anxiety rose in all the humans.

As the cars approached, they could better identify that there were a couple of cars, a pickup pulling a small trailer, and a motorcycle. The entourage slowed down as they got closer to the jeep at the pull-off.

Mac stepped out of the jeep, with his bandana on, leaving the door open as a bit of protection. He raised his shotgun. The entourage stopped before getting too close.

A young man wearing a cap and mask who had been driving, opened the pickup door slowly and raising his arms up high, slowing got out. He turned to tell the others with him to stay still, then side stepped from the pickup to be in the open.

"Don't shoot Dad. It's me, John!". He screamed to be heard over the wind. Again he said "Don't shoot! It is me, your son!"

Mac paused and squinted for a moment. Then he lowered his shotgun and stared. Without turning his head, he said "Mae, I think that's him!" Then Mac pointed the gun toward the ground and started walking toward the young man.

Mae was out of the car in a flash and joined Mac as he hugged their son, all of them crying and talking at once.

Beth watched this reunion unfold, then realized it was okay, lowered her shotgun and walked around in front of the jeep. There were several young men and women getting out of the cars. The motorcycle driver got off and removed her helmet.

Beth walked over to the motorcyclist and stuck out her hand. "I'm Beth," she said.

The young black woman just threw her arms around Beth and hugged her fiercely. "We were afraid we were all alone!" She wiped tears and turned to the rest of the group. Everyone moved in and they hugged Beth and each other. Pretty soon John, Mac, and Mae joined the group and hugged all of them.

"I'm so thankful you are all okay. We were hoping the farm could be a safe place for us to run to," John had tears in his eyes as he said it. "The college and the town were destroyed. We happened to be in a class together that was in the basement of the science building. We had to dig our way out. Jose led us out the storm sewer. It was an awful mess of destroyed buildings and dead bodies. We knew we had to get out of there and managed to find a way to get these vehicles running so we could go. It was a firestorm!"

Everyone was asking questions and talking at once. The dogs and cats were allowed out of the jeep and another group hug was created.

"Hey, everybody!" yelled Beth. "Let's head for that barn behind us." She pointed down the highway they had just driven. "We need to find some protection. There looks to be another clouds of dark grit about to hit us again." Beth pointed at the western sky.

Everyone ran for the vehicles they had come in. Beth's jeep led the way as they drove as fast as they could for the barn. They had to turn down a dirt road that led to the barn, through one broken down barbed wire fence, around some downed electric wires (no power was obvious), across a dry creek bed, but were able to drive up to the large metal shed/barn. It had large garage doors and only a couple of entry doors visible. There did not seem to be anyone around from the outside view. The building had very few side windows but did have solar panels on the roof and some sky lights. There were pens for cattle or horses on one side, but no animals. A large cistern sat on a raised platform between the pens and the building.

"What is this?" asked John.

"It could be a maintenance area, since we are in the National Grasslands. We haven't seen anyone or any sign of people or anything this morning, since we turned off the interstate," said Mac. "We still better be cautious. How about you and I start by knocking on the door?"

John nodded. "Okay", then he shouted to all the cars, "stay put until we see if it's safe."

Chapter 10

Trucker and Marie found a nook in the janitor's closet and waited until they could hear no one around that area of the hallway. The earthquake had subsided, but the wind and grit in the air was heavy and noisy. There were broken windowpanes throughout the hallway. They used the crack of light under the janitor's closet door to determine time of day and waited until it was dark under there before cracking the door to look out. It was dark in the hallway, so listening intently, Trucker slowly opened the door.

The two of them ran quietly down the hallway hunched over until they came to the side of the building. They slipped out the door and slowly closed it so as not to make noise.

Trucker motioned to Marie to stay where she was and he headed to the parking lot full of cars, creeping past each one as he moved toward his pickup. It seemed to take him a long time and since it was dark, Marie had no idea where he might be. Trucker finally showed up by his pickup and tried to catch the inside cab light from coming on as he opened the door. The light flashed on for a second, so he jumped in, started the motor, slammed it into gear, just as two sentinels from the front of the school started screaming for him to stop. They started shooting at him with their rifles. A bullet grazed his pickup bed.

He jumped the parking lot curb and hit the grass, spinning around the building until he reached the end where Marie was waiting. She heard him coming before she saw him, so was ready as he threw open the passenger door. Jumping in, Marie grabbed for the door, just as Trucker slammed the truck into reverse and backing up until he hit pavement. They sped away with tires spinning.

A couple of the guards jumped into cars to give chase but could not get those cars started.

Trucker grinned as he watched in his rear-view mirror. He had pulled the distributer caps in all cars near the front of the school where sentinels had been stationed.

Marie strapped on her seatbelt. "Where do we go from here?" she asked.

Trucker was focused on driving and doing about fifty miles per hour in the school zone.

"Hardware store," he said. "For what?" she asked.

"We are going to need some stuff to get as far as we need to go. There won't be many towns where we need to travel, so we need to prepare for that." He was making a list in his head of what was crucial to have.

The earthquake had created deep cracks in the streets and a few buildings had toppled. Driving was hazardous as Trucker zigged and zagged through the empty street looking for a place to stock up.

"There", pointed Marie as she spotted a familiar sign for hardware down the street.

Trucker pulled up next to the front door of the hardware store, jumped out, and grabbed his tire iron. Walking slowly to the door, he reached for it expecting it to be locked, but it easily pushed open.

Cautiously entering, he scanned all directions up and down the aisles. There were some emergency lights still working, so he could see where he was going. Then he grabbed a cart and moved toward the plumbing section. He caught a movement out of the corner of his eye to the left. He stopped.

A rifle appeared being carried by an old man. He wasn't pointing it at Trucker, but rather at the ceiling. "Can I help you find something?" and he grinned, seeing it was a funny comment at this day, this place and this time.

Trucker laughed and set down his tire iron in the cart. "Sir, we are trying to get to North Dakota and need some stuff for the trip. And, of course, we will pay."

The old guy's eyes lit up. "North Dakota? If you could give me a lift, I'll give you the store!"

Trucker rattled off a list of equipment he wanted, and they gathered it into the cart, dropping it by the door. Trucker dropped a couple of fifty dollar bills on the cashier's counter.

"By the way, my name is Len. I need to grab one thing to take with me," and he went into the store's office.

Trucker grabbed the equipment and placed it in the back of the truck. Marie had a question on her face.

"We have a passenger", was all he said.

Len came out of the store with something wrapped in his coat. Trucker opened the back door and helped Len up into the backseat. Len was very careful with the package in his coat.

Marie turned around to face Len. "I'm Marie", and she offered her hand as Trucker jumped into the driver's seat and they took off.

Len unwrapped his coat and a little kitten poked her head out. He handed her to Marie. Marie hugged the kitten and cooed to it as it started to purr. Len also had a couple of cans of cat food.

"This was the only one I could find after all this started to happen. She's about six weeks, so wanted her to have a chance too." Len smiled.

Next stop was the grocery store. Marie and Len walked into a deserted and dark store with emergency lighting only. She had a couple of large bags and started filling them with staples like flour, sugar, pasta, then went to the canned goods aisle to fill the other with meats, soups, vegetables, and fruit. They grabbed a pot and a skillet from the household section. A few other necessities also fit in the bags. She left cash at the cashier's area for what they got, as well.

Trucker had a new ten gallon can, so he grabbed his portable pump and filled it up with diesel from a couple of abandoned trucks in the parking lot. As he was finishing, he heard a roar in the distance and could smell the sulfur in the air. He knew they were about to get hit with another blast. He hauled the diesel back to his pickup, walked to the cab and hit the horn. Marie and Len came out of the grocery store with their arms loaded, so he grabbed the sacks and shoved them into the back as Marie and Len got into the cab. The kitten jumped onto Len's shoulder with claws bared. She was hanging onto her lifeline.

Trucker sped out of the parking lot, found the highway and headed north with a severe crosswind. He spotted a deep draw on the left ahead of them with a railroad track paralleling the highway. He checked to see that the draw was dry and pulled the pickup into the ditch. He stopped. The noise of the wind was a roar. The truck was sand blasted, but at least it stopped rocking from the crosswind. They had to wait this out.

It calmed enough to allow three exhausted people and a little kitten time to rest and sleep from the last few awful days.

Marie jumped as she was awakened by the slam of the trucks hood. Trucker jumped in and started the engine.

"Sorry about the noise. The wind has died down, but we are getting buried in ash. I had to clean the filter so she will start. We are out of here!" Trucker started the engine, then put it in reverse and spun the tires to get moving. Once they were in a more level part of the ditch, he drove across the highway to the right side and sped up, so they were moving at about 70mph.

"The pickup seems to be running okay. Do you think the wind will slam us again?" Marie only saw the heavy dark haze that surrounded them as they drove along. Looking in front of the truck, visibility was limited.

Trucker was watching where he was going with clear focus. "The GPS will tell me when we are approaching a town. I expect most abandoned cars may have been pushed off the road by the first tornados, like we have seen as we got here. The first wind was worse than it is now and probably picked them up and dumped them in the ditches."

Len sat up in the backseat. "Do you think we can find a place to stop. My old bladder can't hold out like it used to."

Trucker grabbed a large empty cup and handed it back to him. Len took it, looking a bit embarrassed. He handed the kitten up to Marie.

Marie grinned and hugged the kitten. As she turned to look forward, she said "It's okay Len, I was raised with three brothers!"

They drove for about an hour before they came upon a small town, or rather a filling station next to what used to be grain bins. The color they were painted had been wind blasted to the metal they were made of. There were a few cars behind the station, some on their side, others banged up or upside down. The roof covering the gas and diesel pumps had been blown off. A semi-tractor trailer rig lay on its side next to the diesel pumps.

"Let's see if anyone is still here." Truck stopped the truck away from the damages. "I'll check inside and see if the building seems safe to enter," and he walked that way.

Marie and Len opened their doors and cautiously stood up as they got out of the truck. Len put his tiny charge into a small crate to keep it safe in the truck. They both stretched as they looked around at all the damages. Marie pulled up her mask as the soot was still heavy. Len followed her lead by pulling up his bandana.

They walked around in the open space being careful not to get close to the gas pumps, lest they suddenly explode. They suspected that the wind had already done as much damage to any safety devices that existed.

It seemed like it was taking Trucker a while to come out of the building. Marie, wanting to keep calm, just asked "Where are you from Len?" He was about to answer, when Trucker opened the door to the building and wave them over.

They moved quickly over to the front door.

Trucker stopped them before going in. "There is lots of damage and some people died inside so it smells and there is a lot of blood. It looks like there might be a basement or cellar, but I can't find the entrance. Help me look." He pointed to the sides of the building. "Stay together. I'm going to check out the automotive shop next door. Maybe they did what we did back in Pearfish and hid in the pit."

Len led the way with Marie watching her step as she followed.

"I'm originally from Canada. Migrated to Nebraska when my wife and I first married. I lost her five years ago to cancer. We were raised in Somerset, near Winnipeg. Our families still lived around there. I hope to see them again." Len smiled at his memories. "I haven't been back lately as I can't stand the cold!" and he laughed.

"You?" he asked.

"We are from Fillmore. It's a little town near Eagles Lake. Our brothers farm. Our family still…" and she paused. "I hope our family is still there."

They turned the corner of the back side of the building. The roof from the cover over the gas pumps had landed there and broken into large pieces of wood and tin. It lay on top of an old truck. They started to try to determine what might be underneath. It was hard to walk around without tripping on debris.

"Nothing in the garage, as far as I could tell," Trucker walked up as they were looking under sheets of tin.

"I hear something," said Marie.

At first, all they heard was the breeze and smelled the soot in the hazy air, then a 'THUNK'. They all heard it, but with the large area covered with debris they weren't sure where to start looking.

Trucker and Len grabbed a big piece of tin roof and started pulling it away from the building. It was heavy but slid okay for a couple of feet.

"THUNK" came out of the ground under the roof piece.

"I see a cellar opening" yelled Marie. "HELLO! Keep pounding so we can find you! " and she moved some smaller trash away from the cellar door.

"Pull the big piece a little farther, if you can," she said to Trucker.

"I'll get the truck and drag it," and Trucker headed for the pickup, driving it over near them, then backing up. He hopped out with a chain and hooked it to his trailer hitch while Len wrapped the other end around a two-by-four attached to the roof piece.

Nodding at each other, Trucker got in the pickup and Len backed away from the roof piece. Marie stood back from the debris, in case more of it might tumble in her direction. The pickup drug the big piece another ten feet and left the cellar door visible. It was a low slanted door opening into the low side of the building at ground level.

With the next THUNK, the door shuddered. Marie started looking around the edges of the door to see why it would not open. Then she saw it. There was a bolt locking the door shut.

Trucker grabbed a tire iron and slammed it down on the latch. It shattered away from the wood. Marie and Len lifted the door open, making sure the hinges held. Once open they dropped it away from the opening.

Trucker was trying to see what was in the dark hole, when a rifle came up from the dark hold with a small middle-aged woman attached to it. She saw Trucker, Marie, and Len, looked farther around, then she slowly lowered the rifle. She started rapidly moving her hands and making motions, but no noise. Her eyes danced.

The three of them stood dumbfounded. Then Len stepped up. "Wait" and he made some hand gestures, himself. "Slow down", he said as he signed, "so I can remember how to interpret". She stared at him waiting.

Len slowly made hand gestures and spoke as he was doing so. "Hello. I am Len and my friends," he gestured to Marie and Trucker, "have a truck. We needed diesel and food."

The woman started making hand sign quickly, then slowed down for Len to understand.

Len watched attentively and began interpreting. "I am Mary. My husband and I run the store. When the tornado hit, I hid in the cellar. When it quit blowing so hard, I could not get out."

"How did you know we were here?" asked Len.

She signed "the dust fell from the floorboards above me and I knew someone was walking in the store. I used the board to bang on the door, so you would hear me. I did not want to die down there."

Mary started to move toward the front of the building. Trucker touched her shoulder to stop her. She turned and looked at Trucker. He shook his head. She leaned into him and started to cry.

After a few minutes, Marie found a stool and sat down. Len also found something to sit on. They found a place for Mary to rest. Trucker went into the store.

"Several people died in the store. It is ugly in there.", Len signed.

Trucker stuck his head out the door and motioned for Marie to come to the door. He handed her a couple of bags of food and drink. "I'm going to pump some diesel out of the semi over there, then we need to go."

"Okay. I'll see if Mary has anything to take with her, "Marie carried the bags to where Len and Mary were sitting and signing.

"Please ask Mary if she has anything she must take with her. We will pay for the food, but she needs to come with us," Marie waited for Len to sign.

Mary's reply was simply "wait". She got up and touched the door post of the store, then walked in slowly. After a few moments, she came out holding a wedding band, and a bag. She signed toward Len who interpreted for her.

"This is her husband's wedding band as he kept it in the cash register. She said the money will be for when we need things along the way we are going. She said a blessing of the mezuzah." Len took her arm and they started walking toward the pickup.

Marie carried the bags of food to the truck and found storage places in the bed of the truck for the drinks and food he had bagged. Mary and Len climbed into the backseat and he uncrated the kitten handing it to Mary. She hugged and cuddled the little ball of fur.

Trucker brought diesel and poured it into the pickup tank, then went back to the semi and filled the diesel can again, placing it in the truck bed where he had a stationary holder to keep it from spilling.

He and Marie both got in the front seat. Closing the doors, they turned for one last look at the station. Then, looking at each other, Marie said "It is amazing that anyone survived."

The four of them and one little kitten drove on toward the north.

Chapter 11

Mac and John knocked on the doors, then walked around to the window. They peaked in and then waved to the rest of the caravan to drive over closer.

John tried the door, then noticed it was locked with a padlock on the outside. Mac walked to the jeep and found Beth's crowbar.

"The building appears empty, but will give us protection for the night," said Mac. "We will try to bring in the vehicles as well, so we can clean out the air filters and be ready for the morning. Give us a minute and we will open one of the big doors."

Everyone waited in their auto. After a couple of minutes, one of the tall garage doors began opening. Once it was wide enough, Mac walked out and John continued opening the large door.

Mac shouted "drive your vehicle into the building. We can stay and keep out of the winds." He waved and pointed to the motorcycle first, then the jeep with trailer. All others followed.

After unloading just the necessities, Mae and Beth set up a campfire ring with bricks. They asked some of the college crew to try to find something to burn. Wood was best (but most absent) and animal dung would also work. "Don't go too far," said Mae.

Beth pulled out the water and pasta they had, enough to feed the nine of them. She opened cans of green beans, found an onion, and a couple of zucchini. Mae had corn meal in a bowl and was mixing in flour and sugar, with a couple of eggs to make bread.

"We need to soak some of the package of dried red beans so we can make them tomorrow. I have not seen any animals or birds, or we might hunt for some meat," said Mae.

After unloading bedding and essentials, the group began to sit on one side of the fire that had been started to stay out of the way of the cooks. The vent in the roof had been opened to release the smoke.

"How will they find us, or will they find us?" remarked the tall thin student, as the group started discussing their flight. No one answered.

"Leave hints along the way," said Mae interjecting herself into their conversation. She was stirring the pot of stew as it hung over the fire.

"What do you mean?" he replied.

Mac smiled at his wife. "Make memories for yourself and others to share. Your journey is already remarkable. You have already touched others that will share your story, along with their own."

Beth was getting bowls and spoons out for the meal. She stood up and said "first, tell us about each of you. Your name, your life, your aspirations and goals; what makes you, you. I want to know." Mae and Mac nodded and he pointed at the first one in the seated circle.

"Okay. My name is Carmela Cruz and I am from Denver. I am a freshman at CSU and I want to be a nurse. I have three brothers and two sisters and I am the youngest. I got a scholarship and I wanted to be the first in my family to graduate college." Carmela paused. "But now its gone," and she began to sob. The girl beside her who had driven the motorcycle put an arm around her and hugged her tightly. Everyone sat quietly.

"We hope we can find a place for all of us to start again," said Beth. "How about you?" and she indicated the motorcycle driver.

"I am Sydney. I just happened to be in the basement lab working on a genetics project with mice. I am pre-med and this was my masters' project. I had already applied for medical school at Rocky Vista." Mae stopped stirring. "So we have medical minds with us! Do you have family in the area?"

"No. I crossed the wall coming from Omaha. That is where my Mom and Grandma live. I am already an EMT and worked for the Fort Collins Fire Department. I moved west to escape the bias and be able to help anyone and everyone without exclusions."

John was next in the circle.

"How about you John? Does everyone know you and your reason for being in Fort Collins at the science building?" asked Beth.

John grinned. "I am just a freshman and getting my basic biology done towards an Ag degree." He looked around at his travel companions. "And if you have not figured it out yet, these are my parents," pointing at Mae, then at Mac standing by the Jeep, "and our neighbor Beth. I am just thankful we all found each other!"

"Well I am Anthony," said a tall lanky guy with a blond ponytail and some interesting tattoos. "I play basketball for CSU and am getting a degree in marketing. My family is in Utah, and I was lucky to be in the lab when the blast hit the building. I thought the place was going to collapse on top of us. Jose here showed us how to get out. Most of the hallways and stairs were blocked. We had to crawl out through the gutter. It took almost a day to dig our way out."

Jose spoke up. "It probably saved our lives to be in the sewer system. It protected us from the heat blast, the winds, and fire. We could hear and smell, then see the damage after we walked out. That was hours after the first hit."

"What do you do at the university Jose?" asked Mac.

"I manage infrastructure for the college. I was inspecting the water system in the science building. After we found our way out, we went to try to find my wife but our home was flattened," Jose paused. "She had Multiple Sclerosis and was in a wheelchair. I pray she is with God now." He put his face in his hands.

Anthony put his arm around Jose's shoulders.

John reached over to the small young woman and grabbed her hand. "Mini," he said, "you have not told your story yet."

She stood up and stepped over several people's extended legs and sat down by John.

"My name is Mimi Yoshida. I work in the computer lab on the other side of campus. I had driven over to the science building to pick up John. We were supposed to go to the music concert at the stadium. I was early so went to the basement lab to see if he might be ready to go. Thank goodness I was there. Most of the buildings on campus were destroyed and collapsed. I am still in shock at the devastation we witnessed as we left the campus and the city! Hearing the building fall above us was cataclysmic."

John looked at her. "And how lucky we were to get out. My truck was beat up and, on its side, but we as a group managed to turn it back upright. We found the little trailer behind a fallen house near Jose's home. Sydney had gotten her bike to run when we found it on campus. We managed to dig out Jose's car from the front of the science building, though we did have to borrow some tires from a couple of other damaged cars. Anthony found a car big enough for his six-foot frame and we hot-wired it."

"Keeping all the cars running and finding enough gas has been a challenge since we left town heading east. One of the 'tornadoes' pushed us all into the ditch the night before we met you," Anthony said.

"I think it has been a hell of a ride for all of us!" said Mac as he held his shoulder and its sling. "Our barn door blew off its' hinges and would have killed me if it hadn't hit Bessie first." "Did she survive?" asked John.

Mae sighed. "Yes, but when we left, we released the cows and chickens into God's hands, opening the gates at both houses so they could run from the rising waters." She looked at Beth.

Beth stood up. "We had to leave due to the flood waters rising. I also had to leave to find out what happened to my wife and her brother. Contact with the rest of civilization is limited and eventually we were going to run out of food. That was if another of the tornadic blasts did not destroy our houses and barns, first."

"Do you have any idea what happened to cause all of this?" asked Anthony and Sydney almost simultaneously.

Beth explained as best she could what little they knew from the contact on the shortwave. "It seems the volcano erupted in the Yellowstone Caldera, and it seemed to trigger volcanos and faults from Canada and Alaska, all the way down into Mexico. Once they exploded, earthquakes were spawned from the internal heat and violence within the earth's crust." She explained why they were headed north. "We knew we could not go east. South was a story of devastation, as was west. North was our best direction."

Mac walked over to the group. "Do any of you have ideas of what our best move could be from what we know now?"

The circle of people looked at each other, then shook their heads.

Beth stood up. "If everyone is okay to continue together as a group, we need to all have a say. Ideas?" Jose raised his hand. "We are going to need to limit the number of auto's we are driving. We can siphon gas on major highway routes, but it is more limited in rural areas. We should keep the trailers for collecting food and goods."

"I think the motorcycle can be beneficial in scouting areas, so I would like to keep it," said Sydney. "Is it hard to ride in the grit and blasted wind?" asked Mac.

"Yes, but it can fit in one of the trailers if that gets worse and we have room," she responded. "How are we doing for food, Mae?" asked Mac.

"We can do okay for a few days. Since there are nine of us and a couple of dogs, we need to get to a town where we can find food to extend our supply. We will need to hunt for meat if we get to an area where animals had still survived. Even fishing will be hard due to flooding," Mae responded.

"We also need to figure out how to purify water. We cannot carry much with us," said Beth.

Anthony raised his hand. "I saw you have a radio. Can we try to contact other people? I would like to know about my family too."

Everyone nodded.

"We will need to get to higher terrain for the short wave to pick up," said Beth.

"I think we need to eat and get some rest. We will consolidate and leave in the morning," suggested Mac.

They put stew in cups and ate all that was in the pot. Then dividing out blankets and spreading out around the fire pit, they laid down. Mac and Mae's dog laid at their feet. Beth's dog Sami lay next to her. The fire died down to soft snoring and the sound of wind over the tin roof.

Beth sat up with a start. There was no light. It might have been four in the morning Sami raised her nose sniffing the air. It was deathly quiet, like the earth was holding its breath. Then it hit! The slam of the winds, violent shaking of the ground. The skylights darkened even more. Everyone sat up and huddled closer together. Several started coughing from the dusty acrid air they were breathing. They put on masks. The roar of the wind was so loud they had to shout to be heard.

"What do we do?" shouted Anthony.

Mac, John, and Jose got up and walked the perimeter of the barn. The doors were shaking and moving, though they held by their hinges and locks. The roof above the rafters rattled violently. They walked back to the group.

"We need to get ready to move out, in case the building starts to break up. We can stay as long as it protects us but need to be ready if it starts breaking up," shouted Mac. Jose stood up and shouted, "we best prepare to travel."

"Help me pump gas from the cars we are leaving. Pack food and bedding in the trailers. Leave room in the big trailer for the bike," Mac pointed to John, then turned to Mae, then to Sydney.

John, Sydney, Anthony, and Jose followed Mac toward the cars. Mini, Carmela, Beth and Mae worked to pack up blankets and the cooking utensils, food and any water. They all worked rapidly with little discussion as the noise was horrendous. They all glanced at the walls and doors as they worked.

The building held. After about an hour, the blast began to die down. The sky lightened a bit. The winds were not as brutal.

"If there is a pattern, next we will get more earthquakes. Do we leave or stay?" asked Jose.

"I vote we get moving back toward Sterling and catch the highway going north from there. We will have a tail wind until we get there. We should be able to fill with gas. When we cut north it may be tricky but the farther we go the better we may be," said Beth.

"Are we sure we won't need an extra car in case we lose one of the trucks?" ask Anthony.

"Maybe we could pick up another truck along the way in case that happens. They give us better towing power," said John.

"I say we get going, now," said Mae. Others nodded and moved toward the trucks.

They checked outside for any huge cloud of black moving toward them. Not seeing any indication of a fast-moving cloud, Anthony and Jose opened one of the huge garage doors. John drove the pickup and trailer with Mini, Mae, Mac and Jose. Beth had the jeep and trailer with dogs, Sydney, Carmela and Anthony. They agreed to flashlights if either noticed issues or needed to use caution or stop. They had shared some simple Morse code for 'danger', 'stop', or 'SOS'.

The small caravan ventured out once again. Driving east they were cautious of damages to the road from previous earthquakes, or indications of new vibrations. John was leading with Mac navigating. They reached Sterling with no problems and started looking for a location they might fill with gasoline. As they drove through the town, they noticed very few people. The ones they saw were carrying guns. As they reached the outskirts of town, they came upon a car in the ditch. They slowed and stopped behind it.

John and Jose got out a approached it cautiously. There was no one in the car, nor anyone on the highway. They pumped the gasoline out and filled the truck, jeep and two extra gas cans they were carrying. This car was prepared to go some distance, but the air filter probably clogged.

They started north with a crosswind, and some noticeable tremors as they cautiously drove along the deserted highway.

CHAPTER 12

Trucker was intent and focused to get as far away from the horrid winds. Len and Mary were teaching sign language to Marie. The farther north they went the less earthquakes seemed noticeable. There seemed more vegetation and trees standing instead of blown over or charred by fire. There had been fires through much of the grasslands. When they the hit Interstate in North Dakota they headed east. They needed diesel and their best option was a major truck route. When they saw a rest area filled with semi-tractor trailer rigs, they pull off. There were a few trailers laying on their side, obviously blown over from the winds. It was about three in the afternoon.

"Some of the empty trailers got blown over." Trucker said as they slowly drove in. "There are lots of drivers here, which means they do not feel safe to continue driving either way which may indicate a fuel shortage. We will have to approach with caution. Do we have enough food or drink to trade or share?"

Len lifted a six pack of coke and Mary motioned to the back of the bed of the pickup.

Marie pursed her lips, thinking. It had been hours since they had eaten. They had lots of stuff to use for a stew and a big pot to cook it in. "If it is friendly, we could make a big pot of stew and share with them. A bit of food might get us information about the roads and fuel ahead of us."

"Good idea," said Trucker. "You all stay in the pickup. Keep the rifle out and visible." He checked to make sure it was loaded and handed it to Marie with a box of shells.

"I did not know you were carrying a rifle with you," said Marie. "A precaution," was all Trucker said.

The three of them sat and watched Trucker as he walked up to the big rig that was first in the row of parked semis. He stopped before he got too close and opened his arms wide. The cab door slowly opened. A driver climbed down and put on his cap. The two of them talked a bit, with Trucker pointing toward his pickup. There seemed to be some agreement reached as both men nodded. Trucker turned and walked toward the pickup and the trucker with the cap walked around in front of his rig and disappeared from their sight.

Trucker stepped up to the passenger side of the pickup and Marie rolled down her window.

"He said there are about twelve people in the group of trucks parked here. They are happy to contribute to a meal as food is in short supply. They have been here about three days since the world seemed to blow up." Trucker pointed toward the picnic area. "There is a place over there where we can set up a campfire and cook. Sam, the one I talked to will see what the others can contribute."

Marie got out with Len and Mary and started digging through the grocery sacks for foods they could use for the meal. She grabbed a large bowl and big stew pot they had picked up at the last store they had visited. Mary and Len were loaded down with foods as they all carried something toward the picnic area. Trucker had a five-gallon jug of water.

A few guys and gals started walking toward them with some bags. All the group wandered through the picnic area and beyond to find wood to make the fire.

Mary started peeling potatoes from the ten-pound bag they had. Len found a can opener and opened cans that Marie handed to him. The bags from the truckers included peas, carrots, beans and even catsup and mustard. Marie found a large onion and handed it to Mary to cut up. Len started the fire under the kettle.

Marie asked if anyone had any meats, canned or otherwise and someone handed her three cans of Spam. "Aha! This is what Beth would use!" She opened the cans and cut each into chunks. The water started boiling and the potatoes and onions started. After they were on their way to being done, the cans of vegetables and the spam were added. It started smelling good! She wished Beth was here.

More people joined the group around the cooking area. They brought bread and other items to share.

"Everyone needs to bring cups or bowls to put the stew in when it is done," said Marie.

Len spoke up. "Does everyone have water or something to drink?" He sat his box of soda on the table. "I can share this too".

Mary struck up a signing conversation with a burly guy named Earl and they seemed to be enjoying their talk as they grinned and laughed through all their motions.

The aroma brought all fifteen people together in the picnic area. Everyone had found a cup. One of the guys handed out bread to all. They shared it all and the pot was empty within a half hour of finishing cooking. Everyone seemed to appreciate the meal and conversation. It had been the first meal most had eaten during the last several days.

The drivers talked about destinations and any word they had on the radios about travel either east or west. It was clear that south and west were not good travel options. There was word of possible diesel going east, but no confirmation of power to pump it. Most of the truckers knew of manual overrides that could be used to get the diesel pumped. Going north was an option, but mostly farm country, and only Trucker and his companions were headed in that direction.

"We got all the diesel out of the overturned cabs and have shared it around. If you need some, we should be able to fill your tank," said the burly trucker. "Great! We appreciate that," said Trucker.

Marie and Trucker had met a HAM operator among the group and he helped set up the portable antenna and radio in the pickup. They turned it on and searched for contact. It remained quiet all night.

The semi-tractor-trailer rigs started early in the next day as the early sky indicated another blast of heavy winds and grit was heading their way.

Trucker, Marie, Len and Mary, as well as the kitten, also rose early and were loading and preparing to head north when they reached Dickinson. They were unsure of the status of the Missouri River as they would have to cross it, if flooding had not taken out the roads. The semi drivers were worried about the same thing as they are heading for it in Bismarck.

Trucker had also been warned about the border security that had set up in odd cities along the western edge of both South and North Dakota. The truck drivers had said they were mostly vigilantes looking for people to harass and stuff to steal.

A squawk came over the HAM radio unit. "Anybody out there?"

Trucker took the microphone. "This is Trucker Harley. Who are you and where are you?"

Again, came the same question, "Is anybody there?"

Trucker adjusted the channels and the volume. "This is Trucker Harley. Are you there?" There was a pause, then "This is Peace Garden Mike! Where are you?"

"We are mobile on North Dakota interstate heading for Dickinson."

"Ten-four. This is near Canadian Border. We have not heard from west of Chicago since this firestorm started. Where did you come from?".

"Left from near Ogallala, Nebraska a day before the big 'bang'. Got shut down near Pearfish, South Dakota. Storms have been brutal. Is it better near you?" responded Trucker.

"Heard from a HAM trapped in Denver. Word was of major volcano out of Yellowstone and all up and down a line from Alaska to Mexico. Earthquakes split California in half through the San Andreas fault. Countryside is scorched west of Nebraska. Major flooding as dams have broken everywhere. There are continued eruptions and earthquakes. No power as infrastructure has failed in East and West."

Trucker slowed and pulled to the side of the road. "Is there a recovery launched?"

A loud crackle interrupted the connection. "…chaos and insurrection going on. No help indicated."

The transmission ended.

Marie grabbed the microphone "are you still there?" she shouted. He was gone.

"I really need to hear from Beth," she implored of Trucker. "They may have gotten flooded out or worse!"

Trucker took the microphone and hung it on the radio unit. He hugged his sister. "We will try once we get some elevation. That should help our connection. We may hear from more HAMs as we continue north and east. I will extend the antenna as far as safe not to break it. We need to keep moving, now."

CHAPTER 13

John led the way as the caravan had a tail wind until they turned on different county roads and state highways, then onto the interstate once in South Dakota. They would be close to Rapid City, South Dakota. The two-lane road was deserted. They saw few cars or trucks as this was farming and ranching country with national grasslands. There were few towns along the way. As they neared Rapid City they saw more overturned cars and trucks in the ditches with few cars on the two-lane. They were trying to avoid having to cross the Missouri River just yet. Mac who was navigating hoped it had less damage the farther north they traveled, otherwise there would be problems finding ways around. He was planning to take them around Rapid City and northwest to Pearfish where they would hit the state highway going north.

As they reached Rapid City they saw highway overpasses were destroyed on the interstate. They could only go east on the frontage road and followed it along until they saw lots of emergency lights ahead and what little traffic they were following was coming to a halt.

John saw the border patrol truck in the middle of the flashing lights. He immediately took a side street off into a neighborhood. He flashed his brakes with 'SOS' so Beth knew there was serious reason. They found a rather secluded cul-de-sac where houses had burned and were smoldering.

John hopped out and met Beth in the middle of the street. "Border patrol ahead and we are in the wrong part of the country. We must detour around to use some two-lane roads to get to Pearfish. It will help the elevation and maybe give you a chance to connect with HAMs. If it gets tricky, we will have Sydney scout with her bike as I saw she has eastern plates on it."

"Okay," said Beth. "We're with you and need to get out of here."

The two pickups kept close to each other, and everyone was watching for signs of border patrol or other issues. The carefully drove through downtown since it was mostly deserted, then headed toward a smaller town just west of the city. There they turned north again finding themselves in Sturgis. The town of Sturgis was almost flattened. The kept going north on the two-lane that took them through the country. They finally found themselves in the Custer National forest, then were able to cut back to the state highway.

Beth asked for a rest stop on the mostly deserted road. Everyone piled out. The walked around the cars a bit. Some utilized a bushy ditch to relieve themselves. Beth grabbed some snack food from the trailer along with water. They all took a deep breath.

"Anyone want to drive for a while? I need to try make some contacts on the radio while we are still a bit elevated," asked Beth.

Anthony volunteered, so he took the jeep. Carmela was driving the pickup to give John a rest. Sydney unloaded and mounted the motorcycle and was leading the group, watching for border patrol. They were looking for opportunity to get some gas as they had cleaned their air filters and filled both trucks with the spare gas cans they were carrying.

This drive was ugly. There had been massive burn off of grassy areas and still some of the forest areas smoked. The buildings in the area were damaged. Grain silos lay on their side. Barns were flattened. The pavement was cracked and damaged. They did cross some creeks but did not see any flooding in the area. They were still miles away from the Missouri River.

Beth tried several times to get contact on the radio, to no avail. She really needed to hear from someone out there and was ready to start moving east. They needed to find where the devastation ended, and civilization returned. She was afraid of what that might look like as well.

Sydney stopped and waved the caravan over on top of a hill. She stood and looked down on what should have been Pearfish, South Dakota. The water town was laying on its side, houses were leveled and there were random fires burning. The rest joined her and gasped at the destruction.

"Look at the interstate highway," Sydney pointed to the four-lane highway. There were flashing lights from firetrucks, police, and border patrol. Those vehicles had formed a line and had a number of cars stopped. People were being marched down to a school bus.

"I think they are stopping anyone coming in from the Wall to the west and hauling them somewhere in those busses. The so-called police are stripping their cars!" said Mini who had a pair of binoculars and handed them for others to look.

"We have got to avoid this," said Mac as he and Mae started studying the map for different routes.

Beth watched both directions on the highway in case anyone was coming toward them. It was quiet at this moment.

"Okay. It looks like we can head east on the interstate back toward Sturgis, then head north on the state highway. That will take us northeast. We can cut north on any of the state highways or try to cross the Missouri at Whitlock Lake. The river is wide there and more like a lake, though I suspect the flooding will have been an issue. The Missouri is fed by the Yellowstone River in Montana. It is hard to know if there will be anyplace this far west to cross," he paused as he looked at the map. "We might cut across country and try to cross at Pierre."

"We need to decide now," said Sydney. "Trucks moving this way."

They all loaded back into the trucks and Sydney headed the group and led them back toward Sturgis. As they turned off, they came to an RV park where a couple of campers were deserted. The winds had pushed them over and they leaned onto each other and a tree.

Mini flashed her lights to stop everyone. "We need some gas," was all she said to Mac. The group pulled off into the RV park. Jose and

John grabbed the manual pump and the gas cans and set up to pump gas out of the RV's.

"Be careful," said Jose. "There may be electricity on the batteries that can start a fire. We do not want to blow ourselves up!"

Anthony, Carmela and Beth carried each gas can as it was filled to the respective trucks. They had enough to fill both pickups, the motorcycle and enough to fill the gas cans for spare as they traveled across the wide-open country leading to Pierre.

"Let's take some of their fresh water, too," said Beth. "We need to fill those jugs, so we have clean water as we need it."

Mae, Mini, and Sydney took turns filling gallon water jugs.

Mac had laid down in his seat for a bit while the group filled gas and water. His arm was painful from the break.

Sydney walked over to the jeep and tapped Mac on the arm. "I think this might help," she said and handed him two pills. "Muscle relaxers with Ibuprofen. I carry them in my EMT bag."

He nodded and took both with a sip of water. "It was starting to get me down. I just needed to rest for a minute."

Mae walked up. "I think that one of the others can navigate for a while. You sit in the back and nap a bit."

Mini grabbed the map. "I will do it!" and grabbed the front passenger seat.

The rest of the group loaded the motorcycle into the trailer, to give Sydney a rest. Mae put together sandwiches for everyone and handed them out with some cookies and water. They all loaded up ready to keep moving. They agreed to try to get past Pierre before they stopped for the night.

Jose drove the pickup and Anthony drove the jeep. Mini was navigating. Everyone was determined to get as far away from this destruction and uncertainty as possible.

Everyone got into the rhythm of driving and watching an endless sea of farmland. There were more crops growing as they moved east. Beth was working to make connection on her HAM radio. She reached out to Marie and Trucker, her friend Vet Gary, and the endless HAM operators that might be listening. She could get no response.

Suddenly Carmela sat up straight and moved forward in her seat. "We need to switch license tags with another car or truck we pass that is a legitimate Easterner. At least we will not raise suspicion by what license plates we have on our trucks.!"

"Great idea!" said everyone in unison.

"Watch for pickups in the ditch. The tags seem to be specific to type of vehicle. We will still be in trouble unless Sydney is driving, since our identification cards will not be from the East," said Anthony.

"But maybe we are less likely to get pulled over!" said Carmela.

As they neared Pierre, they could see that the Missouri River was outside its banks in multiple places. There was no power to streetlights, so they moved cautiously through intersections as they got closer to the business section. They did see that some businesses were open, but only if they had generator power.

"We need to buy some groceries," said Mae.

Jose slowed down. They were watching for potential markets with lots of cars they could blend in with. He tapped out "stop" with the brakes so the jeep would know his intent. The Jeep responded with "SOS".

Beth had seen police cruisers floating through several parking lots where businesses were open. They were going to have to be careful.

Jose turned onto a road with a sign pointing to campgrounds and the Fort Pierre Grasslands. Not too many people were vacationing during this catastrophe, and he hoped for a secluded space they could stop and stay out of sight. The area was flat, and the river was rising toward the road. With no cover and limited area to turn around the group kept moving with the road. After driving for a short time, the two-lane road turned east and they could see the interstate highway. He slowed to a stop and got out, jogging back to Anthony.

"There is water in the ditch, so we need to mud over our license plates, like we have been camping. If we get on the interstate, we can make better time and probably have a better chance of crossing the Missouri without problem. Mini says we can take the state highway just before Mitchell and find some small towns where we can find groceries," said Jose.

"If we go a bit farther past Mitchell, we can stop in a small town where I have relatives and should be able to get some help from them, to buy groceries, and get a bit of rest," said Beth.

Jose, Beth, Anthony and Mini met between the Truck and Jeep. They discussed the options.

"Well, we have not traveled as far as we wanted, but Mac sure needs to lay down and rest. It would be nice to find someone, like family that would keep us hidden and help us stock up on food. It is still a long way to the Peace Gardens. I guess I'm for going past Mitchell," said Jose.

The others agreed.

"Let's mud the license plates, so we can camouflage our trucks for the interstate," said Beth.

The dogs had jumped out with Beth, and she motioned them back into the Jeep. She showed Mini the town on the map where they would drive. Beth got back in the Jeep. She explained the plan to the group.

"I want to be somewhere there are friendly people," said Anthony. "I want to find family that will make us safe," said Carmela.

Sydney sighed. "I just want to find 'home' wherever that may be." "Me too!" said Beth and prayed 'find the rest of my family too.'

They drove on, hitting the interstate then getting off toward Waterbridge. As they neared the town, the two trucks stopped on the side of the road. There appeared to be no traffic, so everyone got out to stretch their legs.

"I want Sydney to drive me in on the motorcycle. I do not know where my relatives live, so will need to ask around town and scope it out. They will be cautious of strangers, so I want to start out with just a couple of us and go from there," said Beth.

The group discussed it and decided to park the pickup and Jeep up a side road where a group of trees indicated a by-gone homestead. They unloaded the motorcycle. Beth got on behind Sydney.

"Give us a couple of hours. If we do not come back for you in that time frame, get the hell out of here and head on toward the Peace Garden. Canada will be safer than it is here in the East. I pray we find family, but we do not have any confirmation, and I'm a bit low on confidence. Relatives are a couple of generations distanced, so we will find out if they remember family." Beth hugged Mae.

"They will remember," said Mae.

"We will make it happen," said Sydney.

They slowly took off, so not to stir up too much dust.

Entering town, the immediately spotted the gas station. There were a couple of trucks parked next to it and the doors were open to the shop.

Sydney stopped the bike and Beth got off, walking into the open shop door.

"Hi! Anybody around?" Beth asked loudly as she did not see anyone.

There was a screech on the concrete floor and a man pushed himself out from under a car. "Yes, here!

What can I do for you? Don't have any electricity right now but will help in any way I can."

He stood up and a shock of red hair showed beneath his cap.

"My cousin used to own a gas station near here. He died many years ago, but he had family that lived here. I know his sister Jean."

The red headed man grinned and nodded. "I'm his son! Who are you?"

"My mother and Jean's mother were sisters. I am Beth, originally from Texas but transplanted to Colorado."

"I've seen you in pictures! You have a brother who still lives on the family homestead!" He stuck out his hand. "I am Turk! Welcome."

"Yes", and Beth grabbed his hand, then hugged him.

She introduced Sydney. They explained the volcano's eruption in Yellowstone, the earthquakes, the causes of the dark clouds and grit in the air, the devastation from California into Nebraska.

"We had no idea what was going on. We have been without power and communication for three days. We just thought there had been some awful fire or something. I have been expecting deliveries, but no trucks have come this way, yet. Isn't there an emergency Homeland Security plan for this kind of catastrophe?" Turk asked.

They discussed the lack of connection between the East and the West, and the talk of insurrection as this geological event had grossly impacted both sides of the Wall. It also involved Canada and Mexico.

"We need to get back to the group we are traveling with. Is there a safe place we can stay that is low keyed? We have a pickup, Jeep, two trailers and this motorcycle. There are nine of us. We need to get food and water and some rest. After that we are headed north and possibly Canada," said Beth.

"I have just the place. It is a farmhouse outside of town. It belongs to my wife's family, and no one lives there right now. I don't want to worry the town folks just yet about what has happened. Let me get my truck and I'll follow you out to your folks and take you to the farm. You are welcome to stay a few days. I'll stop by my house and have my wife meet us there. Follow me first," said Turk.

They followed him and met his wife, Bev. She was sweet, but confused by the request, so they offered a condensed version of the reason they were here. She jumped into Turk's truck, and they followed the motorcycle out of town to the rest of the caravan.

After meeting everyone, Bev assessed Mac's broken clavicle as she had a medical background. Then the whole caravan followed Turk and Bev to a remote farmhouse about a mile away. It was surrounded by mature trees and vegetation. Bev told them they had been renting it since her parents moved but had just lost their renters.

They parked their truck, trailer, jeep and motorcycle as out of site as possible and walked to the house.

"There is no power anywhere around her right now," said Bev, "but there are logs for the fireplace and the oven is gas and you can cook. There are so many of you, we will get what we can from the local food mart and bring you some staples that you can eat and or carry with you. You can draw water from the well, just boil it as it has not been used for anything but irrigation over the last few years. I'll get some lanterns from the basement."

She started for the stairs and Carmela and Jose both jumped up to follow her and help. Beth pulled out her wallet and handed Turk some money.

"I've got some too," said Mac as he pulled out his wallet.

"This will be plenty," said Turk. "There will be a limit on what we can get from the store, too, since it sounds like our area will be cut off from deliveries for a time. Thank the good Lord for canned goods and generators."

"Please be careful about how much you share of this information with your town folk. There are border agents on all major highways looking to stop Westerners. It appears that the East still does not want anyone to immigrate into their territory," said Sydney.

"Like they care about the ones of us that live in their territory," said Bev as she came up the stairs with Carmela and Jose all holding lanterns, canned peaches, beans and beets.

Beth stood up and took some of the lanterns out of their arms. Mae helped her. "Thank you so much!"

"We still have some flour, so I can make a pie!" said Mae. She headed to the kitchen area to scope out the stove and any pots available to use in cooking.

Turk stood by Bev. "We will bring you what we can about sunset. I need to close my shop and it may take a bit to get someone to open the market. We will bring what we can, as soon as we can."

Beth walked over and hugged them both. "Thank you so much for taking the risk. All of us," and she looked at all the group, "really appreciate your help! These kids escaped with Jose from a devastated city with nothing but a couple of autos and the clothes on their backs. The heat and fires from the blast have killed so many people as well as animals and birds. Flooding is devastating much of the land on both sides of the Rocky Mountains. Thank you!"

Bev had a bewildered look on her face. "We had no idea it was so bad." She looked at Turk. "We are good people and will do what we can to help you!"

CHAPTER 14

Mary had the kitten in her lap and had fallen asleep on Len's shoulder as they traveled along the North Dakota Interstate following the semi-tractor trailer rigs they had shared a meal with the previous day. They decided to continue with the carriers through Bismarck since the caravan offered protection and information if they came upon a roadblock. The truck radios had come alive again as they headed East. It helped that Trucker's pickup had Eastern tags and his drivers' license was official in this part of the world.

As they started to enter the Mandan area the caravan of trucks slowed down abruptly.

"This is Billy Mac in the lead truck. Border patrol have all traffic stopped. They appear to be searching each car and truck, taking things out of each and stashing what they pull. From what I can see, they have some people pulled off and sitting in the ditch. Is everyone credentialed?"

Trucker looked at his sister, Len and Mary. "Do you have any identification with you?"

Len pulled out his driver's license identifying him from Pearfish. He asked Mary if she had anything, and she indicated 'no'. Marie reached for her purse.

"What do you think we can do?" asked Marie as she pulled out her identification that would not be acceptable.

"Give me that ID," and Trucker took it and shoved it in a box of shotgun shells. Then he changed his mind and pulled it back out. "What will they not want to steal," he asked of no one in particular.

Then he slapped a piece of tape on it and slid it in the kitty litter box. "Don't be cleaning that out anytime soon," he said to Len and Mary.

"Marie, you are from Pearfish just like Len. Mary is from that station where we found her. Keep quiet and let me do any talking. We may have to give up some of the food and water that we have stashed in the back. Do not react or fight back if you can hold your cool. They may hurt people if they are just looking for stuff to steal and we make it too hard." Trucker's mind was spinning.

They sat waiting for a while. Finally, a disheveled man carrying a shotgun walked up to the semi in front of the pickup. The driver of the semi got out and walked to the tail gate of the trailer. Trucker got out of the pickup and walked up to them. The driver was opening the trailer gate.

"What are you looking for?" asked Trucker.

"None of your damned business!" the man with the rifle spit out the words.

This trailer was loaded with paper products like toilet paper, tissue, paper towels.

Marie watched the man with the rifle point to a side road, insisting that the driver take his truck over to a parking lot near the stopped traffic. It appeared that trailers were being unloaded or unhooked there.

As the semi was pulling out of line to drive to the parking lot, Trucker started a discussion with the man with the rifle. Marie could tell he was being cautious and congenial. There seemed to be a problem as Trucker kept pointing to the people in his pickup.

The man with the rifle pointed it at the pickup and walked up to the door. He pulled it open and told the three to get out. Len carried the kitten wrapped in a towel. "ID, old man, give me your ID!" was all the guy said. Len pulled his identification out and handed it over. "You both show me yours!" he said to Marie and Mary.

Len signed to Mary what he requested, and she raised her hands and shook her head. Marie handed over her purse but said "I did not have my wallet with me". He shoved all of them away from the pickup. He opened all the doors and dug through bags and bottles that were in the cab, pulling out Len's cola. Then he told Trucker to open the cover on the bed of the pickup. He took all the food and water, then dug through the travel bags and left the clothes in a heap.

After telling Trucker where to take the stuff he pulled from the pickup, he moved on to the next car in line.

Marie, Len and Mary helped Trucker carry all the bags of food and water to one of the trailers that the border patrol group was using to collect the stolen items from the travelers. It had been empty, and the "agents" were using it to haul away peoples valuable food and goods.

They got back to the pickup and waited for the semi tractor-trailer rigs to move as a group. Trucker opened the passenger door and leaned in and started unhooking the HAM radio unit.

"Grab my jacket behind the seat," he said to Marie. "We will wrap this up in it. I'm thinking they will steal my truck." Marie signed to Mary and Len to come close to the door and create a cover for what Trucker was doing.

When he had it wrapped up, he handed it to Marie like a baby in swaddling. Mary put the kitten in with the unit, wrapped in Trucker's jacket. Mary signed "go to truck ahead of us". Marie and Len walked easily up to the driver of the semi ahead of them in line. It was the burly man that Mary had made friends with at the rest stop. He took the bundle and sat it behind the drivers' seat. He lifted Mary into the rig, Trucker was at the other side and helped Len into the sleeper section. Marie got in and the three of them sat on the sleeper bed. Trucker and Earl, the burly trucker, stomped around the pickup and tractor trailer rig, watching others from the vigilante border patrol as they harassed people behind them and a group in front of them were pointing and arguing about what to do with the trucks, pickups, and cars in the stopped group.

Several rifle wielding border vigilantes came down the line of trucks and cars with a group of guys from their crew. They pointed at one of the cars and one of the guys got in and drove it over to the parking area. The family in the ditch started screaming.

They kept coming toward Earl, then told him to get in and get going. He jumped in promptly as his passengers lay low in the sleeper bed and pulled his rig onto the other lane of the highway.

Trucker was already in his pickup as they headed straight for him, pointing and selecting the guy that was to drive his pickup away. Before they got to his window, he hit the gas and spun out heading for the center median knocking the one with the rifle over and side swiping the guy heading for his driver's seat. Several rifles began shooting at him as he bounced through the median and onto the other side of the highway. Trucker kept going.

Earl was moving his rig down the highway slowly as instructed, meanwhile telling his new passengers the blow-by-blow of what was occurring both behind and beside them on the other side of the road. Pretty soon, they could see the pickup as it rushed down the highway going the wrong way and avoiding the few cars coming toward him. The border patrol truck was trying to give chase, but falling short of getting near him, much less stopping him. Len signed for Mary to know what was going on, as well.

The group in Earl's sleeper watched the scene dumbfounded. Len signed and said, "he is going to get himself killed!"

Marie shook her head. "If anyone knows my brother, they are cheering him on! He will make it!" Then she turned to Earl. "Did you two have a plan for meeting up later?"

"We talked about a couple of safe places along the highway. It will all depend on how far he must go to evade the 'patrol'. I suspect it will be sooner rather than later," and Earl grinned.

Since the semi was moving along on the highway without being watched, Mary moved down into the seat next to Earl. The two of them started signing and chatting amicably. Len freed the kitten from the wrap and leaned back against the wall. Marie started organizing the pieces from the radio and began putting it back together.

"We have not talked much about any final destination yet. Is there are place that might be safe for all of us? I have been thinking of Somerset or Winnipeg as I might have some relatives still in that area. I had dual citizenship back in a time that it mattered to anyone." Len was staring out the window as he thought.

Marie looked at him. "I do not know for sure. My brother and I still have family near the border. My concern is to know what has happened to my partner? Is she okay? Where is she? The more we learn about this catastrophe the more afraid I am." She fought back tears.

"We will get that radio working and connect with someone that knows something. The airwaves should start to sound off since we are getting back to the part of the country that is not in shambles. They must get power restored or the people will revolt. Whatever happens, don't lose hope. God has a plan for all of us and love will win!" Len smiled at her and gave her a hug.

Earl was moving his rig along the highway at a steady clip, following closely to a couple of other tractor trailer rigs. "Breaker, breaker, we have a rest stop ahead!" The radio was breaking up badly, but it was starting to work.

"We are pulling off here, but only to see if Trucker has made an appearance. If we don't see him, we keep moving toward Jamestown. That was his plan. Does anyone need to get out for a restroom break?"

Mary signaled that she did need to stop, so Earl pulled into the parking area and parked. Marie got out with Mary, and they headed for the lady's rest room. Marie asked how she was doing using her limited sign language. Mary smiled and hugged her. After using the restrooms, they circled the area to see if there was any food or drink available. There was nothing left and most of the vending machines were trashed and smashed up. They walked back toward the truck parking area.

Earl was standing beside his cab where he had checked the engine levels, cleaned the air filter, and made sure the tires were in good shape. He chatted with several of the other drivers. Everyone had been robbed of any food or drink they had. Word was that Jamestown was very short of supplies. At least they might get water. There was plenty of diesel in the truck tank. They all loaded back in the cab, looked over the parking area one more time and got back on the interstate. Next stop would be in Jamestown.

They made good time and reached the outskirts of Jamestown. Earl needed to keep his rig on the interstate as he was now deadheading back to Minneapolis. A pickup was passing him on his left and going about his same speed. As the driver passed him, they started tapping on the brakes and signaling with his arm out the window to turn off. No one recognized the pickup, but Marie caught a glance of blond hair.

"It may be Trucker! Maybe he had to switch pickups?"

Earl was wary but took the exit which led to a two-lane road. "How am I going to get turned around on this?" he remarked but followed the pickup. After going about five miles they came upon a gravel business with a big truck yard. There appeared to be no one around. Both pickup and truck stopped in the yard. Trucker got out of the pickup and almost fell over.

Marie jumped down from the cab and ran over to Trucker.

"I hurt my leg pretty bad," he moaned. "I wrecked my truck and had to borrow this ride." He looked at Earl who had come over to where he was laying. "Sorry man. Thanks for pulling off."

Marie and Mary managed to splint his leg. Len and Earl helped to get him laid down in the back seat of the pickup. "How do we do this?" said Earl to Trucker.

Marie spoke up. "I will drive. We can lay him in the backseat, and we will prop him up so the leg stays straight."

Mary stepped between Marie and Earl, looked at Earl and Len and started signing. "I am going with Earl. He is headed to Minneapolis, and I have kin there. You (pointing to Marie and Len) will need the room in the pickup to take care of Trucker."

"She is right to try to get to family," said Len.

"I will be glad to take her. My family lives in the Minneapolis area and we can help her find her people. Mary and I have become good buddies over the last day and I can sign again. My mother was deaf! I want to help her find family. I certainly miss mine right now!" Earl was both signing and talking at the same time.

Trucker leaned forward. "Let's get moving. Those border guys will not cut us any slack if we get stopped in a stolen truck." He looked at Earl. "Thanks, man, for all you have done. We will meet again brother!"

Earl helped Mary into the truck cab. Len handed her a blanket and gave her a wink. "Be safe Mary," Len signed to her. Mary waved to them all.

Earl turned the truck around in the gravel pit yard and headed toward the highway.

Marie got in the pickup with Len. Trucker was lying flat across the back seat. Marie started setting the radio up in the cab. She was getting familiar with all the parts and how to reconnect them.

"Stop over at the trailer on the other side of the yard," said Trucker. "What are we looking for?" asked Marie.

"We need an antenna and I saw one over on the trailer/office. It will work and maybe even get us better connections with the radio."

Once Marie had the radio reconnected, she drove the pickup over to the trailer. She and Len got out and examined the antenna. It was bolted to the side of the trailer.

"We need a wrench." Marie stepped up to the trailer door and turned the nob. It opened.

She walked in and spotted a tool belt laying on the floor. She picked up the whole belt and brought it to the door. Len took the belt and found a tool that would work. Marie went back inside the trailer. After a minute, she came out with a plastic bag. "I found some water and stuff." She took the bag and sat it in the seat of the pickup. The kitten mewed from the blanket on Trucker, but sat still. Trucker had fallen asleep with the help of a pain pill that Earl had given him.

Marie helped Len disconnect the antenna and the decided where to mount it on the pickup based on the length of cord from the radio. They managed to get it connected securely to handle the wind as they drove. Marie turned the radio on to test it. "Breaker, breaker," was all she said into the microphone.

Without any notice or static, a response came. "Give me your call sign, Breaker! This is Peace Garden Mike!"

"Oh my word," said Marie. Then she picked up the microphone. "This is Trucker Harley's sister. He had an accident and is resting."

"Glad to hear from you again. You must be getting closer as you are coming in very clear. What is your location?"

"Off of the interstate in North Dakota. Lots of resistance in this area. What do you know?" Marie asked.

"Insurgents stopping motorists on Interstate and stealing goods from families, as well as truckers." Peace Garden Mike explained.

"We were just part of that and now lack most of our stuff. Does it get safer off the interstate?" she asked.

"No word of issue on less traveled routes. Heard it is bad from Fargo to Bismarck. Still little power in rural areas, and no food deliveries, so it is getting tight for residents. Some positive messages coming from the area around Winnipeg. Canada has a response plan and are putting together food and water to send as far as Winnipeg. Farther west than that is limited people, or lots of destruction from volcanos and earthquakes. Heavy smoke fills the airways. This HAM operator has heard of no action for peoples in the states and outside of the twin cities. The only emergency operations of note are in the cities."

"Is the border open to people needing help?" asked Marie.

"Not sure. Have heard that the East US is barring entrance from all directions."

"Need to get moving Peace Garden. Will try to contact you as we move north. Thanks for the information. Trucker's sister, out."

Marie moved the pickup down the road toward the interstate.

"Where do we go?" asked Len.

"We move north via any paved road. I think we are east of the best north/south highway, but if this road gets us to pavement, we will see if it looks okay to go west until we find the highway north. I doubt they are stopping anyone driving into the devastated areas, unless they look like they have something to steal. This old clunker is not going to draw much attention, but we will get off the highway as soon as we can. I am beginning to know some of the towns to which the signs are pointing. Hold on to the kitten. We are going to find good people and safety. First, we need gasoline and to clean the air filter!"

CHAPTER 15

"So, we know where we are running from. So where are we heading? Where will it ever be safe again?" Anthony was frustrated by the conversation around the fire. "I want to know if my parents survived the heat blasts and earthquakes. Can't anybody tell us what is going on. We have no cell phone service, no TV, no radio, no internet. How do we survive? Who can we talk to. Who can we trust?"

The group nodded and agreed with his frustration.

Mac waved his arm. "I know we all want to know about our family, our friends, but we will have to wait. No one in this part of the country knows anything either. They have missed the worst of the damages from fire and flooding, so far, but they do not have power or supplies, or news of what is being done.

Yet they are taking the time to help us."

"I'm going to connect the radio tonight and try to get in contact with other operators to find out what we can," Beth stood up. "We all want to know about our loved ones. We all would prefer to go home. Is there a home for us to go back to?" and she looked at Jose. "You saw the devastation of your home and the loss of your wife. I am sure that does not make it any easier."

Sydney spoke up. "Right now, we are in the East and it is dangerous for us. We are so far able to keep moving north and east with the help of good people and each other. If we wind up in Canada, it would be a blessing, but I bet they too, are having the same issues we have seen in the west. We better pray they will let us over the border."

Mac walked over to put his arm around Mae. "We are glad to be with you all and hope you feel like we are doing our best to guide us to a safe place. Eventually we may get the connectivity that we once could not live without. Meantime, let us continue to work together and support each other in our losses."

"Your right!" said Carmela. "These people are helping us at their own risk."

John put his arm around Mini. "We have each other and survived a lot to be where we are. I am thankful we have made it this far and have a roof over our head for today!"

Everyone stood up together and hugged. Jose was weeping silently in his place on the floor. Anthony helped him up and gave him a hug. "You saved us, man. We love you." All the young people each took a moment to give him a big hug.

Mae, Carmela and Sydnie went to the stove and started dishing out stew. The bread was warm and tasted so good with real butter. John blessed the meal as they all sat back down on the floor. It was quiet for a while as they enjoyed the food.

Beth finished her plate and stood up. "Can you help me to connect the radio to the antenna on the roof, Anthony? I can tell we need your height to get it up there!"

Anthony nodded to her and stood up, handing his plate to Carmela.

"I will help too," said John. "Me too," said Jose.

Everyone else worked to clean up the remainder of the meal, while Beth and the men headed to the jeep to get the parts to make the radio work. They had a small generator too and placed it next to a desk where they could connect the radio to the cable that was strung out the door and up to the roof.

Mini stood next to Beth. "I want to see how you connect this, as it reminds me of some of the electronics I have worked with on a micro level. Maybe I can offer some ideas to boost the reception power," Mini said.

Beth nodded and proceeded to show her what she was doing with the HAM radio.

They had a glow of candles and a couple of lanterns to see what they were connecting. Anthony, John and Jose had scanned the area around the house and reported that nothing seemed to be moving within miles of the house. They settled near the fire and set up blankets for sleeping with the rest of the group. Mini and Beth were working on getting the HAM radio working as the generator was now running and giving them power.

"Breaker, breaker! This is Lab Lady. Can anyone hear me?" Beth started. She repeated this several times without any crackles or noise from the unit.

Mini had a small flashlight and moved behind the unit to check the wiring. After a minute, she handed her flashlight to Beth and said "point the light here," and Mini indicated an area of the internal part of the radio.

Mini pulled a clip from her hair and separated a small pin from it. With the pin, she began probing areas of the wiring.

"I see what is wrong," she said and leaned in closer to the unit. With a minor move to a couple of wires a squawk came from the receiver.

Beth looked at Mini. "is it okay to try to use it now?"

Mini nodded. "A couple of the wires had come loose. Give it a try."

"This is Lab Lady. Do I have anyone that hears me?" There were a couple of squawks and then several responses, mixed together. One response finally came through clearly.

"Lab Lady, Lab Lady, this is Rough Rider. I hear you loud and clear. Where are you located?"

"Rough Rider, we are off the South Dakota interstate. We need news of clear travel. Word indicates that Eastern border patrol stopping anything coming East."

"You hear correctly. Stay off main highways as roadblocks set up at major cities. Truckers are losing their cargo. This is not an organized homeland aid plan. Semis are not able to get west past Rapid City or Bismarck in the Dakotas. Lots of road damages on highways. Flooding all along the Missouri. I am in Minnesota and have heard from a few HAMs in ND and SD, as well as truckers. Limited power in any Eastern locations, and very little word from the West, at all."

Beth paused. "We came from West, and it is bad. We are headed northeast. Any word from Canada? Are they letting people in? We got word we cannot go west or south and know we cannot go east.

North is our only option."

"I have a contact in Peace Gardens. Hold on and will try to get them on." Rough Rider said then their connection with him went quiet.

Beth waited as Mini sat down next to John at her side. Everyone was listening and praying for some good news.

Suddenly a burst of noise from the radio signaled a connection.

"Peace Garden Mike here. Are you on Lab Lady?"

"This is Lab Lady! So good to hear another voice. Rough Rider said you might have information for us as we travel in your direction," Beth said.

"I have talked to truckers mostly being robbed and sent back east. The interstate highway is not safe. Did connect with a couple of folks also heading my way. They were near North Dakota interstate and got off the big highway. Traveling through farm country and beat the flooding at Bismarck. Harder to find fuel. Must keep the air filters cleaned."

"Any more news from the West?" Beth asked.

"Very little communication. Denver was the last place I connected with, and the destruction was apocalyptic. There has been no word on my airways from the west. I have tried Oregon and Alaska, with no luck. It could be power, but I fear it is worse than that. I have not heard from Vancouver or Calgary since the terrific earthquakes and smoke started. Where did your crew come from?"

She sighed, "Colorado mostly. Managed to escape total destruction in Fort Collins and avoided flooding from the area around Julesburg, Colorado."

"This guy Trucker indicated they got hit in Pearfish initially then he got hurt, but his sister is traveling with him towards me," said Peace Garden Mike.

"Did you say Trucker? Trucker Harley?" Beth held her breath.

"10-4. He had got hurt and they were moving north as fast as they could. That was a couple of hours ago."

"I am trying to connect them with the crew traveling with me. If you can connect with them again, tell them there are two trucks and nine people trying to catch up with them." Beth stopped for a minutes and Mae walked over and put her hand on her shoulder.

"Will do Lab Lady. Any other message?" Peace Garden Mike waited. "Tell them Fillmore," was all she said.

"Fillmore, 10-4. God be with you all." Peace Garden Mike signed off. Beth stood up. "Shoot, we still don't know if Canada will let us in."

"At least we know that there are people willing to help us as we move in that direction," said Mac. "Let's get some rest so we are ready to get moving in the morning".

It took a while for everyone to calm down from the excitement of hearing from someone with a hopeful direction in which to move. Beth was relieved and so happy to know Marie might still be moving in the direction with her brother that they might connect soon.

Beth hugged Mini and thanked her for finding the issue with the radio. "Thank God for your expertise!"

Anthony stood up with Jose. "Should we go ahead and take down the antenna tonight? That way we can be ready to move out early."

"Yes," said Beth. "We will need to clean up the place before we go. Thank goodness for the food they were able to bring us tonight. "Mae, can you and Carmela put together a quick breakfast in the morning?"

"Thank God for cereal and milk!" said Carmela.

Everyone settled on the floor for some rest. The dogs would alert them if something came near.

CHAPTER 16

Marie and Len had stopped at a deserted gas station along the two-lane they were driving to the north. Trucker was still sleeping in the back of the pickup as the pain pills were allowing him to rest. Len used the manual pump to pull gas out of the storage tanks. Marie had popped the hood and was cleaning out the air filter.

"Do you think there might be another air filter that would fit this pickup in the station?" Marie looked around the hood where Len was pumping gas. "This one is about shredded."

Len stood up. "You come over and keep pumping gas into the pickup and the spare can. I'll see if I can get in there and try to find one."

Marie moved to the pump and continued filling gas. Trucker had sat up and opened the back door and was slowly trying to get out of the pickup. Marie stopped pumping and walked over to try to help him.

"Are you sure you are able to stand up. I don't think I can hold you."

Trucker held onto the door frame and planted his good leg solidly. "Hand me that old can over there," and he pointed to a plastic bucket that was lying on its side next to the gas pump. Marie grabbed he bucket and took it to Trucker, looking at him for further instructions. "Just sit it down and get back to what you are doing," he said as he worked his zipper.

Marie got the point and went back to pumping gas. She filled the tank then grabbed the spare gas can and filled it up. Len came back to the pickup from the back of the building. He held a bag that was full of stuff, and he was struggling to carry the weight of it to the pickup. Marie ran over to help him.

"What did you find? This is heavy!" She sat it on the tailgate. "Oh jeez! You got water! And snacks!" "And cat food," he said as he opened a small can and put it in front of the kitten.

While the kitten ate, Len helped Trucker back into the back seat. "How are you feeling?"

"Like I have a busted leg. I have never had anything hurt so bad. I cannot put any weight on it!" Trucker was frustrated but pulled himself to a seated position before sliding back into the rear seat with the kitten.

Marie stowed the snacks and water into the bed of the pickup. She kept out enough to give them adequate water and some snacks to hold them over for a few hours. They got back into the pickup, ready for another few miles. "We should be able to make Hazen in an hour. I'm heading there to see if we can get something for your pain and maybe find a doctor to do something for your leg."

Trucker nodded as he sipped some water and ate a cracker. Len was chewing on some jerky.

"How about we see if we can catch anyone on the radio. Len, will you turn it on and make sure the antenna is still connected." Marie turned up the volume a little. Len jostled the wire connecting the antenna and unplugged the connection at the radio, then plugged it back in.

The radio made some crackling noises, the quieted down.

Marie was moving down the highway at a rather fast clip as this part of the country was flat with good visibility. They came over a little rise in the highway and could see a town in front of them, probably ten miles away. "That is Hazen," she said to Len.

Trucker was half sitting up in the back seat. "You better not speed as there is a sheriff there that never sleeps. I bet he will still be stopping speeders, especially with the power being out and having no streetlights."

"You sound like you have had some experience there," said Len as he reached over the seat and picked up the kitten who was sitting on Trucker's lap.

"Too many times to count, even though I learned after the first ticket to never speed there."

The radio squawked. Marie gently adjusted the nobs. Len picked up the microphone. Trucker grabbed it out of his hand.

"Breaker, breaker! This is Trucker Harley. Anyone out there?"

"This is Peace Garden Mike! Been looking for you Trucker. Got a message."

"10-4 Peace Garden, go ahead."

"Fillmore," said Mike.

"Fillmore 10-4. Who sent the message?" asked Trucker.

"Lab Lady, late last night. Best guess was South Dakota somewhere. Crew of nine with two vehicles."

Marie pulled off the road. She had to listen and had lots of questions. "Is she okay? Did she say who was with her. How did she get nine traveling companions?"

Trucker put his hand on her shoulder and went back to the microphone. "Anything more you know Mike, let us know. Thanks!"

"That was the message Trucker. There are big ears out here. Over and out." Peace Garden Mike signed off.

"What does he mean 'big ears?'" asked Len.

"Could be border patrol or other security types looking to snag illegals. We seem to have better connections now, so we need to be careful what we say. Let's get into Hazen and see if we can find somebody to fix my leg." Trucker leaned back and closed his eyes.

Marie drove into Hazen, watching her speed and knowing where she was headed made some easy turns and pulled up in front of a hospital.

Trucker opened his eyes and scanned the area for any police cars or other security type vehicles.

"Maybe you drop me at the Emergency Room, over there" and he pointed to the sign. "Len, you get out and ask the people inside for some help and a wheelchair. Marie, you take the pickup and find a good place to keep it out of sight. Okay?"

Marie drove up to the Emergency Room and stopped in front of the doors. Len got out and was met by an orderly when he got to the door. They spoke briefly and the orderly went back in and returned immediately with a wheelchair and another aid. Len opened the door to the back of the pickup and the two medical types from the Emergency Room gently got Trucker out and into the wheelchair. Len followed them inside after waving for Marie to take the pickup and go.

Marie was familiar with this town and headed to a clinic not far from the hospital. She parked the pickup in the lot with a few other vehicles. After making sure the kitten had some water and the windows cracked to keep it from getting too warm, she got out and walked up to the clinic door. It was locked, but there was a note taped to the door. The note said "EMERGENCIES GO TO HOSPITAL ER".

She walked around the side of the building to an inconspicuous door and knocked quietly. There was no response, so she knocked louder. Nothing happened, so she took off her shoe and started hammering the door with it. The door cracked open.

"Okay okay, I hear you," then the door opened wide enough for a white head to peer out. Spotting Marie, the door was flung open and Marie was enveloped in a bear hug by her mother! The two of them hugged until tears came.

"Get inside," said her Mother and she tugged her into the office. "how the hell did you get here after all this? I have been worried sick. Where is Trucker? Are you okay?" She was full of questions. "Mom, are you by yourself here?" Marie asked, looking around.

"Doc is at the hospital working the ER. I needed to do something since there was no power at home and no phone, and no word. This was as good as I could do." She hugged her daughter again and they sat down on the couch.

"I am so glad to see you Mom. I'm glad you are okay. We have lots to tell you, but for now, we need to make sure Trucker is getting taken care of. He is in the ER with a busted leg. Do you think it is safe to go over there and see how he is doing? You know I do not have papers that make it okay for me to be here."

Her mom got up and walked into the doctors' office. She came back with a lab coat. "Here, wear this. We will walk over there so you leave your vehicle in the parking lot here. Nobody will care since you are with me, but if the sheriff shows up or something, they will think you are part of the care team."

They left through the back door and walked over to the hospital, entering through the nursing entrance that Marie's mom had a code for entry. They walked down the dimly lit hallway and into the ER. The hospital was on emergency power. Marie spotted Len and walked over to him.

"Where did you get the white coat?" asked Len as she and her mother walked up to him.

"Len, I want you to meet my mother, Honey. Mom, this is Len. We found him in Pearfish, and he has become an important part of our trip. How is Trucker, Len?"

"Ma'am," he nodded at Honey, then he turned to Marie. "They took him to xray to see if it is broken. That was right away when we got here. They asked me for information on him, but I told them that he had all that. They have not gotten back to me."

Honey started to walk away saying "I will see if I can find Doc."

Marie sat down with Len. There were lots of people in the waiting room, so Marie removed the lab coat and laid it across her lap. They sat is silence and listened to the other families there with loved ones that needed emergency care.

In about a half hour Honey came out into the waiting room and sat in the chair next to Marie.

"Doc says it is a hairline fracture and he has damaged tendons and muscles. They are going to put a cast on his thigh. This place is pretty busy, so it may be a while before they get the cast on. He got some pain killers and is resting. Do you two need anything to eat or drink? They are offering water and some snacks in the food court. We can grab a table and you can fill me in." Honey stood up.

Marie stood up with her. "We might need a more secluded place. Can we go back to the office and talk there? Len has a kitten in the pickup, and I need to freshen up and even lay down if that is okay."

Honey motioned to Marie and Len to follow her, and they walked out of the hospital through the hallway they had entered. She stopped for a minute at a door and told them to stay still for a moment. Honey slipped in the door, and it closed. After a few minutes she reemerged into the hallway.

"We are good. Doc will have the nurse call the office when Trucker is ready."

They walked outside and across to the physician office building where Honey worked. Marie showed Len where the pickup was located, and he headed over to it to get the kitten. Honey and Marie entered the building and propped the door open a crack to know when he came back. Marie laid down on the couch in one of the offices. Honey let Len in, and they all sat down with some water and crackers.

"I was home when the blast of heat and smoke came through. That was almost three days ago. We had a few rumbles of minor earthquakes, then the power went out. No one in town could find out anything about what happened, but it became apparent this was not a short-term event. We have no radio or television. Will set me up with a generator, but I am only running the freezers to keep food from thawing. He thought it might be a while before we get any power back on. Will and Tess are at the farm taking care of the animals. The cattle were plenty spooked from the earthquakes."

Marie clarified for Len," Will is my brother and his wife, Tess, run the farm near the town where Mom lives. Fillmore is about forty miles from here."

"So, tell me how you got here. I knew Trucker was bringing you. It must have not been an easy trip for him to have wound up with a broken leg."

Marie took a deep breath and started from the morning she had met Trucker for their trip. "It got crazy when we stopped in Pearfish…" and she explained all that had occurred over the last three days.

"What about Beth? Have you heard if she is okay?" Honey asked.

Before Marie could answer, the intercom beeped from the hospital and Honey got up to respond to it.

"This is Mel from the hospital. Trucker needs some extra tests before he is ready to be discharged, so it will be another hour or so. I will let you know when you can come get him. He will need some drugs, so you will have to stop and pick some up."

Honey asked, "Is Doc coming back to the office or should I lock up?"

There was a brief pause. "He said he will not be coming back to the office today."

"Okay! Let me know when Trucker is ready, thanks!" and Honey turned off the intercom.

"When they call I will get him from the hospital. You and Len take your pickup on home, and we will meet you there. It is getting late but I know the pharmacist in town and we will stop for some pain meds for him. I am good with gas, so we should be right behind you." Honey gathered her purse and keys and went to lock the front of the office. They sat and talked for awhile longer until the hospital called. There were many emergencies, so they were keeping Trucker and it would be into the night before he could be released. They had called his prescriptions to the local pharmacy.

"I need to go pick up the pain meds at the pharmacy before they close. You two just rest for awhile. I should be back in an hour or so," said Honey.

"Let me check your air filter before you go. This haze will clog it quickly so do not want you to have any issues getting where we are going," Len said and followed Honey out the door. Marie took the kitten and headed for the couch to lay down. When Len returned they both napped.

Honey returned after a couple of hours and they all snacked and rested until the hospital called. By then it was after midnight.

CHAPTER 17

The smell of eggs and bacon woke the entire group up. It was still dark with no hint of dawn yet.

Mae clanged her spatula on the side of the skillet. "We have this great food to start off our trip today, so get yourselves up and come eat while it is hot. Then we clean up and can get out of here before dawn breaks."

Mac grabbed a cup of coffee and sat at the table. Mae scooped some eggs onto his plate. Anthony and Carmela raised their plates as Mae came close and ate like they had never tasted anything as good. The coffee was where Jose started. Sydney, Mini and John came in from checking the jeep and pickup to make sure they were ready to go. Sydney had loaded the motorcycle into the larger trailer. Beth walked out to the jeep with the radio, followed by both dogs.

Everyone worked together to clean the kitchen, pack up blankets and clean up the area of the house where they had stayed. Mae made sure the bathroom was tidy. Anthony shut the window where they had brought the antenna cable through.

As Beth and Mae stood in the doorway before leaving, Mac walked up to them and put his arm around their shoulders. Then he bowed his head and said "Thank God for this rest and the good people that helped us. Give us safe journey. Amen." They turned and walked to the jeep. All the others were sitting in the pickup and jeep, ready for the next leg of their journey.

Beth drove the jeep up next to John's pickup. "We are taking some side roads back past Mitchell, until we hit the state highway where we will go north. Then we go through Jamestown in North Dakota and follow me through farm country. Mac has the map. Keep eyes behind you for anything out of the ordinary. Use your lights to send a message if necessary. We will not stop unless it becomes absolutely necessary."

John nodded and raised his hand a bit and his pickup passengers erupted with "On the Road Jack and don't you come back." Everyone had a good laugh and smiled as they took off into the dark morning with minimal lights.

As the sun came up there was still a terrific smokey haze in the sky. The little caravan drove steadily, first on dirt roads, then onto paved two-lane roads. They drove under the interstate while still in the country. There was little traffic except a few farm trucks. They drove west for about ten miles before heading north again on the state highway. There were some major cracks in the highway in a couple of spots, so they had to slow down in those areas, but otherwise no problems. The entered North Dakota without incident.

As they neared Jamestown they saw a number of emergency vehicles with lights flashing on the interstate ahead of them.

Beth signaled to turn on a road leading to a wildlife preserve. John followed. They stopped in a small village called Ypsilanti.

Mac lifted his map and said "it looks like this little road should get us past the interstate outside of Jamestown. We will have to stay on it past the Reservoir with a couple of turns along the way."

Everyone got out and took a quick stretch and break. They were anxious to find a safe place to stop, so for now, all wanted to just keep going.

The signs said they were entering a game preserve outside of Fort Totten. They kept driving then turned on a county road near Mondet. The berg of Fillmore showed itself with tall grain silos of the grain elevator, but Beth did not follow the highway into the town. Instead, Beth turned down a dirt road heading north. John followed with his crew.

"Where are you headed?" asked Mac.

"Fillmore is a small town, and we have two illegal vehicles with nine people that are strangers. Marie has a brother that lives on the farm out this way. I am hoping we can be less conspicuous parked near their barn than we would be in the town."

They drove on the dirt road for a couple of miles then the road turned right, with a lake spread out in front of them. There was a house with several barns and cattle pens up ahead.

"This is it. Have everyone stay in the cars. I'll make sure we are welcome." Beth walked up to the back door of the house. When she knocked a dog started barking. Beth turned to her jeep and saw Mae and Sydney holding onto the two dogs traveling with them.

Someone came out of the barn on the other side of the vehicles, holding a shotgun and yelled "Heah" and raised the gun to point it at the sky.

Then the backdoor to the house opened a bit. The lady standing at the door with the barking dog looked at Beth, then at the vehicles with trailers. "Oh my God!" was all she said.

The man with the shotgun walked up to Beth. He wrapped her in a hug. The lady came out of the house and did the same. "Thank God you are okay. We have been worried. Where is Marie?"

"I was hoping that she and Trucker were already here. We were afraid to stop in town yet but needed a safe place to be." Beth waved her arms at the pickup and jeep. "We managed to escape the devastation in Yellowstone and everywhere within five hundred miles of where it started. Our house was flooded. We found six people that made it out of Fort Collins. I think Denver is history." She broke down and cried.

"Can we get out?" asked John.

Will laid down the shotgun on the porch and walked over to the pickup and jeep. "Please get out and know you are welcome. I am Will and this is my wife, Tess." He pointed to the woman holding Beth.

Everyone pulled themselves out of the vehicles. Mac stretched a bit despite his sling. Sydney and Mae let the dogs out and they started barking and cavorting with the beautiful collie from the house.

Anthony unfolded himself from the back of the pickup. Jose walked over to Will. John, Mini and Carmela followed him. They introduced themselves, shook Will's hand, then hugged each other.

"We had no idea where to go. It has been a long trip. At least we now have a flicker of hope," said Jose.

Tess brought out bottles of water and handed them out to all these travelers.

Will wanted to know more. "We have not had news or power for three days. We had no idea what created this mess. What the heck happened?"

At first everyone started talking at once. Mac waved his good arm to calm and quiet the group. "We all have pieces of the story, so it may take a while to share. Beth, you start with what we know from the radio operators we have heard from."

The discussion went from the eruption in Yellowstone and the trigger effect on other 'extinct' volcanoes from Alaska to Mexico, the subsequent earthquakes, the news of the Andres fault splitting California. The Fort Collins group talked about the huge heat, wind, and fire of the tornadic bursts as the fire wave tore through Fort Collins. Beth told what she heard from Denver before they were cut off. Mac and Beth talked about the heat tornado as it hit the farms. Beth gave her view of the flooding that shut the roads off to the east as the dams broke from the earthquakes.

Will took a deep breath. "We knew something had to have caused the earthquakes, and we have had quite a few. The cattle are spooked, so we rounded them up so they would not stampede and get lost running through fences and getting hurt. It is no wonder that there is such a smelly and gritty haze. I have not been near Eagles' Lake in the last three day, nor has Tess, so I do not know of any dams that have broken here."

"There were indications that the Missouri had flood damage as it reached Bismarck, but we did not see much in South Dakota as we tried to get past it as soon as we could," said Beth.

"We have just been without power or communication for the last couple of days. Mom went into Hazen yesterday morning to see if she could help at the office. I better drive to town to see if she got back okay. I had a generator running to keep her freezer and fridge running. I need to take in some gas to fill it up. Sounds like this is not a short-term power outage." Will stood up and stretched.

Tess interrupted the chatter. "Do you know if Trucker and Marie are anywhere near here. They should have driven in for a visit yesterday. They could have gotten caught up in this mess."

Beth sighed. "They had a HAM radio when they left, and I have tried to contact them. We have not had any luck. There was word that the Interstate was a hotbed of border patrol taking down truckers and stealing their cargo. It would make sense if Trucker got in the middle of some of that since those are routes he knows well."

"Tess, please help these folks set up in the basement so they have a place to rest. I'll be back in a little while once I figure out what Mom knows," and Will walked toward his pickup.

Tess stood up and motioned to the group. "Bring your stuff and I will show you where you can settle in."

Mae walked up to Tess. "Is it okay if our dogs come in with us?"

"Oh yes! They can come in. Just don't let them tangle with the cats!" Tess grinned.

"Where is the best place we can get the jeep, pickup and trailers out of sight?" asked John.

Tess pointed past the barn. "Pull them over near those trees by the barn. There is room and they won't be seen from the road. Will can have you move them when he gets back if there is room in the barn."

Everyone grabbed their meager belongings and the food that was left from their trip. Sydney took the keys from Beth, and John walked with her to the vehicles. They moved them out of sight as directed, and Sydney removed the motorcycle from the trailer. Then they walked back to the house.

The rest of the crew followed Tess into the house carrying the few things with which they had arrived. They were all exhausted.

John stopped to survey the farmland. "It looks a lot like our place in Colorado."

Sydney paused as well. "If I did not know better, I would think I was back in Nebraska." "Thank God for farmers!" they said in unison and laughed.

Tess pulled meat and beans from the freezer, and grabbed canning jars full of tomatoes, pickles, beets, and jellies. Mae and Beth grabbed some of the things from her hands and followed her back up the stairs.

Tess turned to Carmela and nodded her head toward the freezer. "Grab a couple of loaves of bread, Hon. We will need that with dinner."

Carmela opened the huge freezer that Tess had just been inside. "Wow! I have never seen such wonderful options. You must have half a pond of fish and a whole beef frozen in here!" She pulled out a couple of bread loaves and closed the lid. "I want to help! Coming from a big family, I want to see what you make to feed so many of us!"

Tess grinned and the three followed her upstairs to the kitchen.

Once stew had started boiling on the gas stove, the aroma lured all the rest of the visitors from the basement. It smelled wonderful. Everyone helped arrange enough chairs around tables, set out paper plates, bowls, and utensils, and followed Tess's instructions as she coordinated the meal plan. She had already unleashed Mae on making a couple of pies.

At one point in the operation, Tess put her arm around Carmela. "When you have three boys with growing appetites, you have to try to fill them up. I'll bet that guy," indicating Anthony helping move chairs, "can put food away just like my boys!"

It was a wonderful meal of beef stew with potatoes, onions, carrots, peppers, and rich beef broth from the flank steak she had included. The pies were out of the oven and waiting for them once the main meal was finished. Everyone helped clean up once the meal was finished.

"Hey, everyone!" said Beth. "We need to talk about our next steps, so go ahead and walk off some of this wonderful meal and we will meet downstairs in the open room in a half hour—say seven o'clock."

The sun was going down as everyone did take a short walk, pet the kittens in the barn, admired the land and the lake. Jose and Anthony were talking basketball; Mac and Mae were strolling and holding hands; John and Mini laughed and giggled at each other; Sydney and Carmela chatted about friends and family.

Beth caught up with Tess on her boys and how they were doing. Will had yet to return from his mother's house in town.

At seven everyone had found their way to the basement and seated leisurely in a circle. Tess listened from the stairs. Beth took a deep breath before she began.

"It has been a hell of a few days for us all. Thank you and thank God for getting us here in one piece. Thanks to Tess and Will for offering us a warm and safe place to stay." Everyone clapped and hooted.

"Now for the hard part," Beth looked at everyone, one at a time. "What do YOU want to do next? We must decide where our new safe place is going to be. These people are wonderful and part of my family, but most of us are still illegals without permission to be here. I suspect the governmental repercussions will not be accepting, despite the horrendous disaster from which we have escaped.

Sydney may have more choices as she has credentials to be here. The rest of us need to find a new home where we can be accepted and safe, and more importantly, free."

"Why can't we stay here in this little town?" asked Anthony.

Tess spoke up. "Our law enforcement here is all about keeping out illegals. Farmers and ranchers have been threatened with jail time and fines if illegals are found on the farms. There is also a bounty that many farmers use to help their own poor cash flow."

"So think about where you want to go," Beth continued. "Do you have family or friends that will take you? Do you have connections through work, school, or talents that will give you an edge? There are the twin cities in Minnesota. Canada may be an option, but we do not have confirmation that they will let us in to apply for asylum. This devastation has taken a toll on all of our neighboring countries.

Survivors of the West will all be looking for a way out, just like us. We may be a part of what few have escaped, but all of us need help to re-establish ourselves in a new place. I do not think we will be able to go back to the home we once knew for a long time."

The group was silent for a bit.

Anthony stood up. "Well, I know I want to play basketball, whether in college or professionally. I have talked to agents in Ontario, as well a Chicago. I can probably get in touch with them again. I miss my family, but don't know if anything is left in Utah…"

"I lost my closest connection to family when I lost my wife to Multiple Sclerosis and that damned wheel chair. I have relatives in Minneapolis," said Jose, "but I think I would like to explore options in Canada. I need to learn about who I am in this world without her".

Mae hugged her son and looked at Mac. "We are farmers and though not young, have our talents that can be very useful. We are thinking about trying Canada."

"I miss my family too, like Anthony. This trip has showed me more about my resolve to be a nurse. I am ready to try new places and discover how I can help people. It will make my family proud!" Carmela had tears in her eyes but a set to her jaw showing her resolve.

John moved over close to Mini and took her hand. "Mini has taught me to reach for the stars since she has overcome adversity that her family has been subjected to."

He looked at Mini, so she turned and continued. "They lost their farm and were sent to Japanese internment camp during WWII. My granddad fought in Germany for our country. He became a lawyer and had his own firm that my dad continued as he grew up. I was able to get my master's in information technology and had been offered a teaching position at several colleges."

"She has also been sought after by companies from finance to insurance to protect their data bases!" said John proudly.

"What about you, John?" Mini looked at him and asked.

John looked at his parents. "I had already decided to move from agriculture to engineering after my first year in college. Waiting to start after high school for a couple of years was a good thing for me. I got to work for Marie's company and learned lots about solar. I want to get into design of larger solar systems. Between the two of us, we want to be able to reconnect with the world through advanced education, advanced technology, and the development and usage of non-fossil fuel power for our world. We could start in Canada." He grinned.

"Sydney! You have been awful quiet," said Beth.

"I have been listening and thinking. I love my family in Nebraska and miss them, but that is not where I want to be. My heart is in medicine, and I want to be a doctor. I had applied to Medical School in Minnesota and was accepted there as well at Rocky Vista in Denver. I wanted to stay in Colorado because I had met the love of my life and she was already established in banking in Denver. I need to know what happened to her…" and Sydney sobbed.

Beth put her arm around Sydney. "I'm missing my right arm, too," Beth said.

Sydney took a deep breath and gathered herself. "From what we know right now, I am open to anyplace that will accept us and let us be vital, contributing members of the community of mankind. We must change how we treat our world and value it or we will manage to kill ourselves as well as our natural resources. If it takes a catastrophe such as this one to get our attention, then we better be listening. I am so proud to know each one of you. I am ready to try new places and new things."

Tess had listened and watched from the staircase as the group shared. She heard a car drive up as Sydney finished, so she went up to check the driveway. It was Will's pickup and another old beater- bomb beside his in the drive. Will was helping someone out of the backseat. Honey's car drove up and parked behind the beaten old pickup. A grandfatherly man stepped out of the old pickup and brought out a small kitten. Honey got out of her car as well.

Will supported Trucker as he got balanced under his weight on one leg with a caste on the other leg. Marie walked around the back of the pickup where she had grabbed a couple of bags.

"Let's get him inside," said Honey.

Honey watched her two sons as they hobbled up to the back porch. Marie went to Trucker's non-casted side, and he put his loose arm around her neck. Will supported his weight as they took the three steps up onto the porch.

Honey brought up a walker and put it in front of Trucker. She looked at Tess. "Where do we put him?"

Tess led the way down the hall to a bedroom and Trucker followed, dragging his casted leg as he slowly followed her. Will helped Trucker sit down on the bed, then swung his legs gingerly onto the bed until he was laying down. Tess tucked some pillows under his head and took his cap.

"I'm good," was all he said as he laid back.

Will and Tess walked back into the kitchen. Honey introduced Len.

"This guy hitched a ride with Trucker and Marie in Pearfish. This kitten has been dubbed Volcano," and she laughed.

Marie hugged Tess.

"Will said you had a house full! Where are they?" Marie looked around, then up from the basement came Sami who rushed Marie and jumped up on her wildly. She patted and rubbed the Collie, then came Mae and Mac's dog, also requiring hugs and pats.

Beth poked her head up from the stairs. Then she ran up the last few steps, rushing into Marie's open arms. "Thank God you are okay!" both said as they held each other tight and buried their heads in each other's neck.

Chapter 18

"So, what do we do next?"

The whole rag-tag group of refugees sat together in the basement of Tess and Will's home. They had rested, laid low, enjoyed good food and some relaxation had come over a day. They had talked about the last few days, their pasts, their dreams and their fears.

Will had reported that the sheriff had caught him at the post office in the little town and asked if he was expecting to feed an army. "The grocery store said you almost cleaned them out! Do you have family coming for a visit or something?"

Will had responded by laughing. "Nah," was his reply. "My sister and brother are coming for a visit if they can get here through all this mess. We were planning to celebrate our mom's birthday and have all the neighbors. Since it has been hard to get anything these last few days, I figured I had better stock up with what I could find, including lots of beer."

They had laughed about having a good reason to celebrate something right now. "Don't let anyone drink and drive!" and the sheriff left to do his county rounds.

Will reported this interaction with the group in the basement. Everyone was somber and thoughtful.

"I talked to Peace Garden Mike just an hour or so ago. He believed that the Canadian border patrol is accepting people from the West, but there have not been very many. They have taken some to an interim holding facility. Our best opportunity to get in is to have some form of identification. With that we should be able to apply for asylum. There is no guarantee they will take us." Beth pointed to Len. "Len has dual citizenship, so maybe he can vouch for all of us."

Sydney spoke with decided confidence. "I'm good to stay here in North Dakota and Tess suggested trying to get into the Medical School at UND. They are hurting for doctors and nurses. Carmela might have an opportunity too, if they are willing to help get her cleared to stay." Sydney was becoming more sure of her destiny than ever.

Carmela nodded. "I have a good start to be a nurse, can work as an LPN and if they are looking for that and will let me stay, I'm ready to try."

Beth looked at the group. "So if the Canadian border patrol will allow us to apply for immigration, does everyone else want to head in that direction?"

"I'm with you!" said Marie.

Mac and Mae nodded their heads in unison.

Jose spoke next. "I have always wanted to represent a basketball player and I think Anthony may need a representative. I know of some opportunities for him in Canada, both college and pro."

Anthony nodded. "If they let us in, I can try out wherever there is a pro team, unless a college might pick me up for next fall. I need someone to help make all the contacts as I am not real well spoken. But my aim is to play, so I'm going to look for opportunities!"

John and Mini stood up. "We have talked about it and want to get a fresh start in Canada. Mini and I want to stay together and find our spot in this new world."

"Trucker will go back to trucking, I assume?" and Marie looked at her brother.

"Hell yes! And I've got to get me a new pickup!"

Everyone chattered about their ideas for the next move. After about ten minutes, Marie stood up and whistled! "Hey everyone! Let's talk about the steps we need to take. The sheriff is asking about too much food, so we need to clear out of here quickly. Tomorrow morning would be a good time to head for the border. You that are staying in the East may need to wait until there is better communication about what is going on with electricity, gasoline, food and supplies."

Marie turned to Sydney and Carmella. "We have a niece that might take you in until the college is open. She will have some connections at the school, too. Can you get there on the motorcycle or should we try to get you a ride?" The three of them started talking about logistics.

Beth asked, "Will you help us with getting into Canada, Len?"

"It will be my pleasure! After all your Marie and Trucker did for me, I am happy to get my relatives to take you in!" Len grinned. "I am excited to see my family again, too." His kitten Volcano purred.

"Okay. We will have to take both the jeep and the pickup since there are nine of us. We will have our best luck if we head for the Peace Garden entrance to Canada. Maybe Peace Garden Mike can help us with the entry. We will need to keep our plates in low profile in case we meet the sheriff. Should we drive up in the dark, then wait until they open in the morning?"

"Try to contact Peace Garden Mike and see what he says. He may know more about your options," said Trucker.

Beth and Marie went upstairs to get on the HAM set. As they got to the top of the stairs, they saw the flashing police lights coming up the dirt road.

"Police!" yelled Marie.

Trucker was working his way up the stairs. "Stay downstairs with lights off and be quiet. Let me see if I can defer some of the heat!"

Will, Tess and Len helped Trucker into a recliner off the kitchen. Tess went to the door and opened it, waving to the Sheriff in the police cruiser.

"What's going on Sheriff?" Tess asked.

"One of your neighbors said there was an illegal beat up truck in your drive. There were a couple of other notices about illegal vehicles coming this way from Mondet. I see the old pickup and it is listed as stolen," said the sheriff.

Tess brought the sheriff into the kitchen.

"Afternoon Sheriff," said Will.

"Who is driving the 'beater bomb' in the driveway?" the sheriff asked, looking around at Trucker and Len.

"That would be me sheriff," said Trucker. "I wrecked my pickup just off the interstate when I broke my leg. I needed to get to the doctor, so I 'borrowed' it. It took so long to get out of the emergency room, and I got drugs, so I could not get it back to the owner, yet."

"Let's see your ID," said the sheriff. Trucker handed it to him, and he studied it for a second. "And I see you are a CDL driver."

"I am the one that took the pickup sheriff," said Len, and he produced his driver's license. "This man saved my life in Pearfish and since he was injured, I found the pickup and took it. He needed a doctor badly."

The sheriff rubbed his chin. "These are strange times," and he paused as he thought. "The old guy that notified us that you had illegal trucks here was a little tipsy. Maybe he remembered it wrong. When can you get it back to the owner?"

"Right away sir. Right away!"

CHAPTER 19

Beth and Marie sat outside under the stars watching for the Aurora Borealis. They held hands and rested in the quiet of the summer night. It had been a wild ride over the last week, and they had no idea what to expect at the Canadian border.

"I hope we can stay together," said Marie. They had no idea how people would be handled at the internment camp.

"We are a family! Why would they separate us?" said Beth.

They enjoyed the moments then went to join the rest of the group to finalize plans for leaving.

"Looks like we are leaving tonight," said Beth in low tones to the group. She turned to Trucker. "Should we take the 'beater bomb' and dump it in the country before we get to the border?"

"No. Just leave it be. I will drive it back to where I got it, then hitch a ride at the truck stop. They will get me back to Omaha in a couple of days. You all need to get moving tonight though. I wish I could help."

The jeep and pickup had only the necessities in them and were still a bit crowded with five people in one and four in the other. The dogs had been left on the farm with Will and Tess. The kitten was still with Len as he would be able to enter Canada once they verified his identity as having dual citizenship.

Peace Garden Mike had indicated that the rest of the crew would most likely be taken to a holding facility to be processed. Everyone had something that could be used for identification. Those without official documents had letters from Trucker, Len or Sydney with their identification as verification of who they were and where they were from. These letters could be traced to verify who each person was once the internet was working. It could take some time.

As they drove up to the border patrol station near the Peace Gardens, everyone took a deep breath.

"Here we go," sighed Beth. The jeep she was driving took the lead and pulled into the waiting gate.

A Canadian border agent stepped out of the booth, noted there were two vehicles full of people, with tags identifying them as Westerners, and waved to another agent to join him. The agent then waved both jeep and pickup drivers to park next to the entry booth. "Please get out of your trucks," he said pointing next to the booth, "and stand over here."

By the time everyone had gotten out of their vehicles there were four border agents watching the group.

"We are seeking asylum," said Marie. "We came from the West after surviving the fire blasts and earthquakes. We want to come to Canada."

Everyone nodded their assent to her statement.

The border patrol agents led the group into the administrative building near the entry station. Each person was searched and produced whatever identification they had. One at a time, they were interviewed and their request for asylum was documented.

Len also had to go through this process, as data base information was not available. They let him keep Volcano with him.

The agents explained that they too had many disruptions since the initial firestorm. Earthquakes, and distant eruptions had torn down power lines, interrupted commerce, created flooding, and disrupted all forms of communication whether phone, or data. They also told the group that the Canadian government was accepting requests for asylum from the people of the West. They had limited resources but had very few requests.

"We do not know much about the situation of the peoples of the West, except that there was massive destruction in many major cities. Most of the information we have received came via short wave radio. We have also had very little commercial traffic from the East, so our commercial resources are quite limited. You will all be taken to an interim holding facility until your information and identifications can be processed. There you will have food and shelter. We cannot guarantee how long this process may take, so please be patient."

The agents placed their pickup and jeep in a parking lot. "You can get your autos once you are permitted to stay."

They all got into a small bus and were driven for several miles to the holding facility. It looked like a large gymnasium with a fence around the outside. There were a few people walking in the open area inside the fence. They stopped to look at the newcomers, as the bus was unloaded at the front gate.

The woman in charge of the facility stepped up to the new group. "Welcome to Canada! I am Anna La Croix. Please follow me." She led them into the building.

It was a large gymnasium with a high ceiling and huge open floors. One area seemed to be set up with cots and blankets and there were already some people that had settled into a part of the area. There were some children playing, some people laying in their cots. Across the room looked like there was a kitchen area. There were signs pointing to bathrooms and showers. There were several doors that opened to the outside where people were playing ball, some people were hand washing clothes and there was a clothesline where sheets and clothes were drying in the wind.

Many of the adults walked up to the newcomers. "Where are you from?" "What happened in your part of the country?" "How did you make it this far?" "Can you tell us about…?" The questions went on and on.

The next several days were filled with stories of horrid earthquakes, awful burning winds, blinding ash storms. Few people talked about seeing their homes destroyed, but rather in not being there when it happened. Families ran for their lives. Many were traveling to or from their homes when the blasts happened, or earthquakes hit. Most were able to hide in underground shelters, like schools or as with Trucker and Marie, in underground pits. Some were blown off roads by the tornadic winds. Some lost parts of their family in the trip. All were running north and east, just like the winds were blowing them.

Marie and Beth finally had the time to catch up. So much had happened to each during the last week. It seemed unreal that so much could happen in such a short time. They mourned the loss of their home, their animals, their garden, and their peaceful life. They wept over the losses of their friends and other family. They prayed for guidance and direction in this whole new day. They reveled with joy over having found each other again. The thanked God for having survived with their new friends during crazy and unknown times.

One morning Anna came to find Beth and Marie. "I have heard that you have a short-wave radio. Is that so?" she asked.

Beth replied "It is in the jeep that was left at the border when we came in. I should be able to get it to work if the border agents could bring it to us."

"Okay," said Anna. "We need something to reach outside our area. We need medicines and even a doctor if we could find one. Many of the townspeople have come down with some kind of sickness that is worse than the flu or Covid."

Marie piped up. "At least start with wearing masks to slow the spread. Please consider keeping people from town out of here, too. We are an isolated community and if it starts here it could wipe us out."

"How would we feed you?" asked Anna. "Our staff live in the community".

"We can cook and clean for ourselves," said Beth. "Just deliver food and supplies. We will figure it out. But bring the radio from my jeep. The guards may have to help erect an antenna and share messages, but we can keep safe, and still make contacts for healthcare."

Anna stood with her hands on her hips, thinking. "Let me talk to my boss at the border patrol and the mayor. We will get the radio. I will pull my staff out right now, except for guards. They have a shed to protect them during their shift but will need to assure everyone stays put. Can you organize all the people in here to take care of your needs?"

"Just give us access to cleaning and cooking supplies and we will do our best to clean and isolate ourselves from whatever is going on in town." Marie was thinking where to begin. Marie took the keys to the kitchen and the storage area from Anna.

Beth grabbed Anthony and Jose. Anthony let out a loud whistle. Jose went outside in the yard and did the same. They had everyone inside the building within five minutes.

"The town has come down with a virus. We are going to need to take care of ourselves. First we must clean to prevent spread by anyone that has worked here over the last couple of days. We must prevent getting this virus inside this compound. We need to wear makeshift masks in case anyone here has been infected already. Even the children. If no one comes down sick, we should be able to stop wearing a mask after five to seven days. What say you??" Marie had spoken and looked around the room. "Remember Covid? This must be a mandate. We need to set up cleaning schedules and cooking teams. Everyone must help."

There was some grumbling, but everyone got the point and began volunteering to help. Teams for each duty divided into functional and necessary areas. Mae was designated cook team lead and Mac led the kitchen cleaning crew. Beth took women's bathroom and shower cleaning. Jose led the men's bath and shower cleaning. John and Anthony led the crew to assess stock items and fuel. Mini took on laundry and gathered a crew to help.

Beth and Mini found a stack of clean sheets and with the help of their two teams of volunteers, they cut squares to use as bandanas. John found the cleaning supplies and dispersed to kitchen, bathroom, and general area cleaning. "Wipe down anything with the chlorine solution that someone could have touched or breathed upon."

"Anyone with a sniffle, cough, runny nose, or just feeling bad; come see me!" said Marie. "Hey, John! See if there are any medications in the staff or storage rooms. May at least need some aspirin and a couple of band aids!"

Most everyone worked hard to do the initial cleaning. Anthony became the pied piper for the children and made a game of wearing masks. Mae had dinner going with her crew by the time the cleaning of all areas was winding down. Mini had already started washing to keep up with laundry re-supply and John had the generators running for some lights by the time for dinner. They also shared lanterns and candles around the huge room.

Len surrounded himself with children and told stories to them that made them giggle and wiggle. Four of the men volunteers to be security and held a vote to see what time was "lights out". A woman that had been a nun offered to read the bible and have prayers in the evening. Another teacher took a sheet and a couple of candles and set up a puppet show. Everyone offered something they knew how to do to make their time here bearable.

The following morning border patrol brought the HAM radio. Beth wiped it down, then worked with Anthony and Jose to set up the antenna. She contacted Peace Garden Mike quickly.

"No word that the virus going through White Rapids' water is serious. Will contact doc in Winnipeg and get meds sent down. How is everyone at the compound?" Peace Garden Mike inquired.

"We are wearing masks just in case, but no illness so far," responded Beth. "Who is cooking?" asked Peace Garden Mike.

"Mae is our best. We get homemade biscuits every day!" said Beth. "I think I need to move in down there," laughed Mike.

"Get those meds to town and we will invite you to breakfast!" said Beth.

"A promise is a promise, Lab Lady!" and he signed off.

After a week, Anna presented herself with her staff at the entry to the Canadian border holding facility.

"How is everyone doing in here?" she asked tentatively.

The two security detainees grinned. "Well, we like the cooking better since we picked our own cook.

Maybe Mae could share some tips with your guy," he said to Anna and laughed.

He let them in the entrance area and Anna led the way for her crew. The detainees all met them as they entered.

"Is everyone well?" asked Marie.

"We are," said Anna. "The doctor investigated and after talking to the city water people found they had not adjusted chemicals in city water to accommodate the issues created by flooding. You were all okay as the water out here is from a well."

Everyone was glad to be done with another potential problem and panic.

"I have one release order," Anna said. "Mr. Len Monet has family that have vouched for his birth and heritage in person. They drove down from Somerset and are here to pick him up."

"My family is here?" Len said. He hugged his kitten and his eyes got misty as he strained to look beyond the group of staff and security.

Anna turned toward the door and asked her security to bring his family inside. Len moved toward the door with his kitten sitting on his shoulder.

As three people entered, and Len's eyes widened. "Franny," he cried, and the older women ran to him. A younger man and woman moved toward them. He hugged them as Franny introduced her son, Mike Schotz and his wife, Milea.

Marie and Beth were right there grinning and so excited for Len. Marie put her hand on his shoulder and looked at his sister and family. "This guy is special!" she exclaimed.

Len introduced his sister and her family to all his travel companions. "This is Marie and she and her brother picked us up in Pearfish. This is Beth, Marie's wife that found the rest of these friends as they all ran from the fire, quakes, and flooding. They all lost their homes and livelihood." Everyone chatted for a bit, then it was time for them to leave the compound.

"Help us get out if you can Len!" shouted Marie as they left.

At lunch, Anna came to the dining area and stepped up to the podium like she was going to make a speech. She began "We still have no internet to verify you and consider your requests for asylum. But since all of you have been so helpful to our little town, our merchants and farmers would like you to consider an offer they have discussed. They have about twenty jobs that they have no candidates to fill.

Now these are basic labor job—cook, dishwasher, plow hand, secretary, and a few manufacturing jobs. I have the job descriptions. Anyone that would like to apply, can do so and if hired will be allowed to leave here every work day to go to that job. You can continue to stay here, eat here, and sleep here, until your request for asylum has been approved. I have posted the jobs on the board next to my office. All interested can fill out an application and bring them to me." She stepped down.

There was an immediate rush to see what jobs were available. Most all the adults crowded around the board to see the options. Everyone wanted to be productive again!

CHAPTER 20

The West lost more than half of their population in the devastation of the last weeks. With California split with the Andres Fault breaking open and being engulfed with part of the Pacific Ocean, the total loss was unknown. The flooding of major metropolitan areas due to dams rupturing created much loss of people, but also of electrical power and clean water. The commercial supply chain that much of the East and West depended upon was totally shut down. Ships had sunk in tidal waves, docks had been destroyed, and there was no way that commercial trucking could function well as highways were severely damaged. Railroads could not deliver either, as tracks were broken or destroyed across the continent. The Wall had been inundated by what few survivors that could make the journey toward the East, but the Eastern border patrols refused them entrance. Canada was accepting Westerners but could not confirm people's identity or background and had few resources, just like the East and West of the States.

The Eastern government was on the brink of collapse, as military leaders threatened a coop. Leaders in the Western government had not been heard from as they were in totally devastated metropolitan areas. The ocean front properties across the world were now underwater. The weather was no longer predictable and there were no public broadcasting methods that could have power and connectivity to reach even the smallest portion of peoples to warn them of more danger.

The Americas, both North and South were not alone in the catastrophe. The rest of the world had also been met with chaos created by the earth's crust cracking open as the molten lava from inside the earth's crust was exploding in any opening it found. All the peoples of the earth found themselves working in survival mode to simply feed themselves and find safe havens to protect themselves and their families. New smaller communities of peoples formed and held together to survive as they tried to recreate an environment that was viable and sustainable. People all over the globe were relearning how to live one day at a time, and where to find food and water, as well as shelter, if they were to survive.

The weather was wild, but at least the summer sun made environment warm enough to sustain survival in the northern hemisphere. The coming of fall and winter would bring new and more dangerous challenges, especially in the northern part of the Americas.

CHAPTER 21

The refugees being detained near the Peace Gardens in Canada were safe and have been provided for during a difficult couple of months. All were weary of not knowing how their lives could move forward in the midst of so much being unknown where they were isolated in Canada. The people working the detention facility did not know any more than they did. Some inkling of the total world impact was starting to be heard on the minimal communication airways.

Anna La Croix brought the entire group of detainees together one evening to offer an update on their status. "We have found out that our government does not have a timeline when information can be provided in order to legally release you into the Canadian Provinces. They do know that workers are needed to try to restore internal means of survival. You will all be issued temporary Visas and be released to find work outside of our small area. Our focus has to change so that in smaller grouping of peoples we can restart producing what is needed for survival. This also means that you will have to find your own shelter, food and water. We no longer have the means to support your wellbeing. Talk to your employers if you are currently working. There will be a bus for those wishing to leave the area that will take you into the metropolitan area of Winnipeg where you may seek jobs and housing."

She continued. "I am sorry our world has changed so violently. We would help you if we could, but our resources have been depleted. Our families will also be seeking refuge in different ways until we find some new level of normalcy."

"You will only have a week to ten days to move as this facility will be shut down indefinitely."

Supervisor La Croix had tears in her eyes, as did all the residents and the workers in the camp. She stepped down from her podium slowly. The detainees opened their arms and wrapped her in warm hugs. They understood how hard this was for everyone.

The group of eight sat down together in a circle to once again discuss their plight and make a plan, if possible.

Each of them had been working at jobs in the area. Marie and John were working at a local factory making farm equipment. Mae and Mac worked the morning shift at a little café, cooking and cleaning. Beth was doing phlebotomy at the local hospital. Mini was working with the Canadian Mounted Police to try to get them reconnected with their leadership. Jose had been working with the city to reestablish their water supply and keep it safe for drinking. Anthony was a janitor at the local school and was also working with the school coaches to develop the younger players in soccer, tennis, track and field, and basketball. All the jobs were vital, but not necessarily sustainable to provide the refuge that the area was going to need going into the fall and winter.

"When Len was here last, he mentioned that his nephew was a farmer. Do you think there is any chance we might offer ourselves to expand their production and grow a wider variety of crops? I think they were mostly focused on wheat and had some cattle." asked Mac.

Jose shrugged. "I am not a farmer. I do believe that my job will continue with the city to maintain the water supply. At this point, I might be able to get my plumbers license again."

Anthony raised his hand. "I love working at the school but could do without the janitorial work. I think I want to go to Winnipeg and try to connect with the college there. I might get a gig working with the local high school to make enough to eat and have a place to sleep, maybe in the dorm."

"I could probably tag along with you and see if they have need at the college for a good 'plumber'," Jose offered. "Then I might help you get back on a team and still go pro some day!"

"Marie, what would you say about starting a solar plant?" asked John.

Beth and Marie looked at each other. "Maybe…but where? We need lots of resources for the parts and the frames. Those might be more available in Winnipeg, if they don't already have such a plant."

"I have not seen any solar panels on any homes around here. They seem to have plenty of sun in summer but would need batteries to store energy. And homes would need supplemental heat during winter. I think some currently use wood or coal to supplement electricity." Beth was trying to verbalize a picture of homes that operated off the grid.

John and Mini were quiet for a little bit. "I bet you would need someone to design, market, communicate, and install those panels. I still want to get my engineering degree, but I would be willing to help such a company. How about you Mini?" said John.

"I am okay to work in that industry, but where do we get the resources to even think of starting a company like that?" Mini replied.

"Let's slow down and step back, maybe even as far as our great grandparents," said Beth in a thoughtful manner. "We had to do some of this after the Wall was built and infrastructure had fallen apart. We brought food resources together. We used hidden resources to recreate industry as well as government. Healthcare was unavailable, so we went out and either found medical help or found those that would come and live among us. We must start from the beginning, and that is food and shelter!!"

"Maybe we could live in the Shotz's barn. I bet there are lots of people that still can vegetables and fruits so we could help gather and do the work. The gardens are just starting to produce. We could ask for a portion of the foods for our labors, then trade what we do not eat for chickens or cows. With those we can provide eggs and milk to trade for other needs." Said Mae.

"That is a lot of canning, but the idea has great promise. We could eat healthy and probably some of us could do some hunting for meat?" said Marie.

Jose grinned. "Do we know if they have a barn that we could live in for a time? I hear it gets bitter cold in the winter here."

"Well surely someone would have a place we could live, even as a group. There are probably many old homesteads that are abandoned here, just like we saw in South Dakota. I know this is also true in North Dakota and Texas. The Shotz's family would know of these kinds of places near them," said Beth. "We could work for Mike if he needs help and trade our labor for other resources."

"Ok," said John. "We need to do some investigating. Beth, can you contact a radio operator that might help us communicate with Len's family?"

"Yes! Len gave me information on a HAM operator that lives near his family. I'll get on it," said Beth. "Start writing ideas and questions down. Mini, do you have access to maps of the area between Somerset and Winnipeg?"

"I think so," said Mini. "What am I looking for?"

"Solar related businesses or warehouses," said Marie as she winked at Beth, and grinned. "We have to see if current resources exist."

Mac stood up next to Mae and helped her up. "Well, it sounds like we have some ideas of where to start. I can still drive tractor, milk cows, and fix plowshares. As long as Mae has something to cook, I am all in!"

Everyone laughed and nodded in agreement.

"I am still going to the college to apply and find a job there, and hopefully play basketball," said Anthony, "but I will help in any way I can, too."

"Hey! I am still going to be your agent, man. It will just be a work in progress! Our first step will be to get you enrolled and push for a scholarship to pay for your education. You will need a career 'post-basketball' someday," and Jose grinned.

Communications through the radio operator near the Shotz's farm proved very helpful. 'Phil the Pill' was the HAM operators' handle, and his family homestead was vacant and still standing. It was within several miles of the Shotz's farm. He was to share all the questions with Mike and Len so they could get some answers for the group.

"I think my Mom still has canned goods in the cellar, and I know the well is good. There may even be a good cook stove in the place. Not sure about the electricity though." Phil paused for a moment. "Oh yes, and my grandad's old tractor is still in the barn. I have no idea if it still would run. There may be some varmints that have moved into the barn. No one has lived there for a couple of years."

All the initial information that the group received gave them a place to start planning.

The Canadian border patrol released the jeep to Beth and Marie, as the title identified them as owners, while the pickup was released to Mac and Mae, as they were listed on the registration.

Everyone was given a temporary Visa. Anna explained that they would need to reapply in a year with the Canadian government. She hoped that by then they would also be eligible for application for citizenship.

"I am proud to know you and can say I have never met better or more hard-working people than your group. Welcome to Manitoba, Canada. Keep yourselves safe," were Anna's parting words.

CHAPTER 22

The eight newly released survivors with their temporary Visas in hand drove the jeep and pickup with their meager belongings to the community of Somerset. There Phil was to meet them to guide them to his homestead. Len and his nephew Mike were also planning on meeting the group at the postal office in the town. The surrounding area was fertile farmland from what they saw. The terrain was fairly flat, but here were multiple creeks, ponds, and even lakes through the area.

They parked on the street by the postal building, got out and stretched, and chatted for a few minutes until a pickup drove up. The driver was grey headed and rolled down his window.

"What the hell do you think you are doing here on a Sunday? The Postal is closed. I don't know who you think you are, but I will make sure the constable will check you out and maybe throw you out for loitering around here." He spun his tired and left abruptly.

Everyone was standing there and watched him leave. Their mouths hung open.

"Is it the license plates on our trucks?" asked Anthony.

"Or should we be in our 'church clothes' and dress up to meet the towns' people?" added Mae.

The group did look a bit rugged as their few clothes were worn and tattered, though clean, thanks to Mini and Beth.

After a few minutes, another pickup drove up to the group. A tall skinny guy pulled himself out of the pickup and waved to the group.

"Hi, I am Phil. You must be the Westerners from the immigration camp?"

The group walked toward him in a leisurely manner but stopped when a police car came rushing up to them with lights blinking and a siren blasting.

The officer got out of his car with his hand on his gun. "Everyone just step back and show your hands! Now!" he yelled.

"Hey Constable," said Phil. "These are the folks from the immigration camp that I told you about." He walked up beside the officer.

"Bill Johns came by the office and said they were casing the postal office. How well do you know these strangers?"

"Well, I do not know them yet, but Len and Mike," and he pointed to the incoming truck and continued, "are friends of theirs and have vouched for their intentions."

Len and Mike got out of the truck they had arrived in and walked up to the constable, having heard Phil's last statement.

Mike spoke first directly to the constable. "You know my uncle Len just got back here from the Western US?"

The Constable nodded. "So?"

"So, these are the people that saved him from getting blown away or burned by the catastrophe that just happened back a couple of months. My wife and I along with my mother met all these folks at the refugee center when we got Uncle Len," Mike explained. "Phil, here, has agreed to rent them his family homestead—what is left standing—so they have a place to stay. Some of them are going to work for me on our farm."

The Constable finally removed his hand from atop his gun and looked at Mike, then Phil. "So, you are vouching for them then?"

They both nodded as did Len.

"I still want to see their identification and Visas, otherwise they cannot be here." The Constable held out his hand to the group.

After studying each visa and whatever other identification they had on them, he said "Okay, but there better not be any trouble. People cannot just come into our province looking like something the cat dragged in and expect us to welcome them with open arms." He huffed off and got back in his police cruiser.

He looked at the outsiders and with a sweep of his arm out the window of his cruiser said, "if I hear of any troubles around here, I am looking for you people first." Everyone gathered around Len, Mike and Phil.

"What did we do wrong?" everyone shook their heads.

"I should have remembered to wear my suit and tie," said Mac. "Does no one around here know what happened back in our part of the world?"

Phil shook his head, as did Mike. "We still have little information being shared by our government. Most everyone still has no radio or TV, and some are still without electricity. We are all tired of having few groceries in the stores and have no information to understand that the world blew up."

"Yeah, and we are spoiled into thinking that everything will just go back to the way it 'was before'" said Mike. "I'm just praying we can get ourselves prepared for winter before it comes."

Len had stood thoughtfully for a moment, then he said "I have begun to believe that what people see right here, or their lack of what they see, is being blamed on the 'states'. Somehow they think that the East and West caused all of this, and the folks here want to blame someone."

"Do you think it will be safe for us to live in your family's homestead for a while, or should we try to find somewhere else?" asked Marie.

"Let's give it some time. Our best opportunity might be to go down to the church right now. Could you talk about your experience in getting here Uncle Len?" asked Mike.

"Sure! I would be glad to share. Maybe some of the college folks could talk about surviving by being in the sewer and managing to meet up with the rest of us!" said Len.

"I can tell them what I have learned on the radio, so they have a summary of what really happened," said Phil. "I had not thought it would be important to people, but guess I was wrong."

All four vehicles drove to the only church in town. The windows were all open and the congregation was singing. The whole group of eleven walked in the church door and up toward the front. The pastor stopped and stood there for a moment. Phil headed to where the pastor stood and whispered in his ear. Phil then took the pulpit.

"Most of you know me as my family has farmed around this area for years. I am Phil Pilsner. I am also a Ham radio operator, and it is through that communication that I can give you a summary of what has been going on over the last couple of months to give us what we are living through today."

Phil started with the Yellowstone caldera exploding and its expansion to massive volcanic activity from the artic all the way through South America. He gave examples of other radio operators that were near destruction and their descriptions of their surroundings. He explained how the railroads in Canada had been brought to a halt by earthquakes and floods, how there was no electricity as lines were torn down and dams that were creating electricity could no longer do it. Phil did not cover all that he had heard, but his synopsis got to the heart of the matter when he explained that Vancouver was practically under water as the seismic faults had broken and allowed the ocean to pour down their streets. He also explained the forests in western Canada continued to burn from the volcanic ash. He was in tears when he stepped down.

Then Jose stepped up to the podium. He introduced himself. Taking a deep breath, he told the story of his and the students escape from Fort Collins, including the part when they stopped to see his home collapsed and his wife crushed. "We are a people with just what we have on our backs. We will work hard and become productive members of your community, your province, your country. Many of us will want to make it our own, and we will do so by giving of our skills, talents, experience, and ourselves to become valuable members of your country."

The Constable had walked in at the beginning and had sat down next to Bill Johns during the testimonials by Phil and Jose. They both got up and walked up to the front to shake hands with the eleven strangers that were now more welcome to their world.

CHAPTER 23

The old Pilsner home was a huge rock house that had weathered more than a century of Canadian winters. The family had kept it tight and safe for years. The new immigrants were determined to appreciate and care for this fortress as they determined and prayed about how to start their lives over from this new place.

Phil helped Beth get her antenna and HAM radio set for usage. Marie had put together a solar panel that would provide sufficient power to run it. Phil told her that the connection with the HAM operators across the world was the best communication that the world had right now. It was crucial for all of the operators to share information and determine what the whole world was experiencing and living through. It was also crucial to share information so that commerce, could get restarted.

Phil immediately asked if Marie could make him a solar panel as well. "Petrol is in short supply, just like everything else." She said that she, John, and Mini would get him connected.

"Phil," asked Marie, "where is the best place to get information about available electrical equipment and available plexiglass? Any ideas are welcome. We can build panels but must get more parts to put them together and then allow them to connect to batteries or electrical units of low voltage."

Phil thought about it as they were walking out of the house and into the back yard toward the barn. Mac and Jose met the group as they were coming from the barn.

"We were looking to see if we could fix up the barn, and as we are able set up a chicken coop and a small coral for a cow. The roof needs some work, but the walls are sturdy!" Mac was excited and ready to get his hands back to work, since his collar bone seemed healed.

"I can see how to connect the water well back to the windmill," said Jose Mac said he could repair the structure, so it stands high enough to catch the winds. "The trees will have to be trimmed, but we think it can be done!" Jose was also getting excited to create a sustainable environment.

Phil raised both his arms. "You people need to get to work, I think!" He laughed. "This place needs lots of work and my family has little to offer to help. The rent we get from farming it out does not cover much. You are on your own to rebuild anything."

"Will it be okay to use what we can find? How about if we need to tear down that old shed," and Mac pointed out beside the barn. "Some of the wood is good to reuse. That will also give us some nails and should be doable!"

"Go ahead. I figured we would eventually just have to burn the house and barn or tear it down. If you can create something from nothing, more power to you," said Phil. His family was letting them stay without charging rent, for the present.

"We will still ask before tearing anything else down. We will have Beth contact you over the radio," said Jose.

Anthony and Mae came out of the back door off the kitchen where he had been reaching high into the cabinets to retrieve old pots, pans, dishes, glasses, and even old flatware. Now the whole group was talking at the same time about opportunities they saw around the old homestead and were well aware they would be making something wonderful out of the resources at hand.

Phil started waving his hands. "I must get out of here and get to my job over in Winnipeg. I will look into the stuff you asked me about in regard to plexiglass and electrical. I will contact Beth when I get any information. Have her contact me with any questions about the place. I wish you the best! This was a fine homestead when I was a boy and I would love to see it back in the form that my grandparents kept it."

Everyone waved as he drove off in a cloud of dust. Anthony whistled "Shreeeeek"!

"Okay everybody. We need to make a priority list of where to start. Jose says that I have a couple of months before it is even possible for me to get into the college in Winnipeg. I am going to need a basketball court!"

Everyone talked at once, so Anthony again whistled, "Shreeeeeek".

"I think we remember how to work in a democracy, so maybe we start with a list by everyone, and after we eat some dinner, we can have a meeting by the fireplace." He paused then looked at Mae. "We found the pots and dishes, so who is cooking and what are we cooking?!"

Beth and Marie went to the jeep and brought back a bag of groceries that Mike and Len had given them before going back to their place. It had dried beans, pasta, flour, sugar, salt, soda, powdered milk, a can of lard, coffee, and a huge bag of potatoes. As they put it inside the kitchen, Marie hugged Mae, then said "okay what else do we need to find or create to make this work to feed us for tonight and a few days longer?"

Mae pursed her lips and squinted her eyes in concentration. "See if you can come up with some eggs. Maybe down by the pond. Duck eggs are great so we will need to protect the ducks and feed them so they stay around until we can get some chickens. Tomorrow, I can bring up what canned goods are still in the basement and see if any of it is still edible. Mac needs to set some rabbit snares and see if we can get some meat. We will want to save the hides and dry them to use later. Somebody is going to need to go fishing. We have enough salt to brine some fish…" She was digging deep into her memory to find what was needed since all the conveniences of the last hundred years were not available to them here today, in this place. They had no money to go to any grocer to even see what they might still have in stock.

"And have Anthony see if he can find a pail and a rope, so we can draw some water for tonight. We may have to boil it to make sure it is not contaminated. I will get the old gas oven to heating."

Mac, Anthony, and Jose came up with the pail and rope and brought up water for the kitchen, then some more for everyone to wash. Mini and John were peeling potatoes. Beth and Marie were out near a pond in the reeds looking for duck nests and had some old grain to lure them. Beth had made a cane pole and tied on some fishing line to create a fishing pole. She used a safety pin she found for the hook. They had set it on a rock after finding some juicy worms to use on the hook. She had no float but estimated the depth of the pond by wading out into the water with a stick about a yard long. She and Marie continued their egg hunt, then returned to the pole. When they got there a large fish was trying to swim off with the pole. She managed to snag the pole and pull in the catch. She reset the line and waited, this time. The fish were hungry this evening! It was dark by the time they returned to the house with five duck eggs, and six good size fish.

There were whoops of joy from everyone when they saw the catch. Mae smiled. "Wonderful! God provides again! Thank you, Lord!"

For the next few weeks, they managed well on these blessings. The ducks, fish and rabbits provided them eggs and meat. John had gotten a job driving a combine to harvest wheat. Mac was driving truck for the combine crew, as was Beth.

Anthony and Jose were busy fixing what plumbing they could repair, and Mac was rebuilding the windmill. Anthony had relived his childhood and climbed every tree near the well, trimming and cutting large branches. All would serve as fuel for the fireplace as it got colder. Mini, Marie and Mae worked on cleaning the house while discovering usable cloth, brooms, soaps and brushes. There was an old treadle sewing machine that still worked. Most of the canned goods from the basement were not salvageable, but they saved the wax and the jars for possible late summer canning. They did find some seeds and cut up some potato eyes and had planted the garden area after Jose turned the dirt with a hand pushed plow. With some water from the well, lettuce and spinach came up quickly. They were soon followed by squash, cucumbers, onions, peanuts and potatoes.

About a dozen ducks had taken up residence near the barn, so they had eggs every day. Marie had shown Mini how to use the cane pole, so fish became a staple in their menu. Mae had shown them both how to brine and smoke the fish, so it kept without refrigeration for a day.

Jose had discovered a wild berry patch out behind the barn. He also found a beehive during his search and was very careful once he knew where the hive was located so as not to get stung. There was a book in the old house on bee keeping, so he and Mini were deciding who was brave enough to use what they learned and harvest some honey. Mac had laughed at them and on a rainy day, had gone with them and shown them the art harvesting honey, using smoke to stun the bees.

The harvesters earned pay for their work and as the harvest crews were moving out of the area, they brought home baby chickens and a cow. Other money had been sent to Phil for to purchase needed equipment to work the farm, as well as electrical materials, plexiglass and framing materials for solar panels. Marie, John, and Mini had designed the process to construct and produce the panels once they got adequate supplies. Another issue they had thought of was placement. The snow would have to be pushed off the panels or they would have to be almost perpendicular to the ground and raised high.

Snow cover in this part of the world was often quite deep. This was a huge creative discussion around the fireplace as the evenings became cooler.

By the end of fall with winter coming, the house and the barn were once again in good shape. The water well provided clean water and they had solar panels set near the house and barn with a means to change the angles for weather and best collection. They had been able to purchase electrical energy storage batteries for use with solar.

The barn had become a small manufacturing plant for solar panels. The cows and chickens shared part of the space, so good ventilation was important. Marie and John were hiring workers to increase production as the result of Mini and Beth creating an advertising campaign. Communications were beginning to come back online in the Canadian provinces. Mini was working with the Somerset community to get their internet back online to reopen communications, education, and faster information sharing. Transport had renewed the area with supplies they had survived without for a really long summer.

Anthony and Jose had traveled by bus to Winnipeg to get Anthony into college and he was recruited the day they first walked into the athletic department of the college. Jose even found a job with the college directing their infrastructure maintenance and updating. They were starting where their lives had left off, in some ways. The immigration experience after survival from an awful experience had changed both men. Anthony had a keen sense of gratitude for everyone and no longer assumed he would get what he wanted, but knew he had to earn it. Jose became open to new learnings and new opportunities. He now worked with Anthony as if he were the son he never had. They were a solid team.

John and Marie had discussed how to expand the solar panel operations. They needed to include the whole group in the planning.

"The old barn is not going to last forever and if we expand the manufacturing, we will need to be closer to a larger labor pool, easier transport of supplies, and faster shipping of products to customers. We have a good start and could borrow the money to set up in a better location," said John.

"You mean we have to leave this old house with all it has given us these last months?" asked Beth.

"Unless you want to buy it and drive to work, I am not sure there is a choice," responded Marie.

Mini jumped into the discussion. "Well, our children will need to be closer to school in the wintertime. I am ready to get back to civilization, movies, theater, shopping!"

Conversation paused as everyone needed clarification to part of Mini's statement. Mae eyed Mini and John closely. "Is there something you are not telling us?"

"Mom, Dad," said John as he stood up, "Mini and I want to get married. We want to start our family. We are ready to have our own place and raise a family like you raised me, with love, honor, integrity."

He leaned over and kissed Mini on the forehead. "But of course, we will gladly skip repeating the 'adventure' part of this last year. "

"The business that all of us have created will do better near a larger city and we will get a broader interest in what we make. Marie, it is your creation, but we have all made it work. How about a partnership of the six of us?" asked John.

Marie stood up and hugged John and Mini. "John and I have talked about this a lot. Beth and I have thought about the possibilities and problems. Mini, are you on board for us to invest in a place in the city?" Mini smiled and nodded. "Mae, Mac, you have a stake in this in a huge way. Shall we all move and create our business in a new place? Can we continue to be like family?"

"As long as Mae makes biscuits and Mac takes care of the honey," Beth chimed in.

CHAPTER 24

They continued their lives at the Pilsner farm. The demand for solar panels was increasing steadily, so keeping up was difficult. They had good workers, but the winter weather often made it hard to get them to the farm. The same problem made it difficult to provide the product to those ordering solar panels for power.

Talking about creating a manufacturing business and actually doing it was not an easy process. The group had multiple problems to overcome. They had to reapply for their Visas, then apply for citizenship. They had no credit history, except for a few months in the Manitoba province, buying small amounts of electrical equipment and parts, along with plexiglass and framing. They paid their bills with what their clients paid them for the products they built. They owned no property, except for cows and chickens that allowed them to sell milk and eggs to the people in the area. They paid rent to the Pilsner family. They were able to save some money and were establishing credit history. Unfortunately, the length of their stay in this country, and still little credit history did not make them attractive customers to the banks.

Beth and Marie stayed in contact through the HAM operators as often as possible reaching a few that survived in Colorado, western Canada, Texas, and Mexico. They were able to get news of the little progress being made in the West to restore and control waterways. Production of electricity had been partially restored through wind and solar power, but so much of the infrastructure had been destroyed that getting power to the people was a huge challenge. Commercial products were still not readily available as trucking was limited; the roads were in some cases irreparable. Railroads were working to repair their tracks. The challenges of rivers being out of control created more problems for rebuilding bridges for all roads and railroad tracks.

Beth had HAM contacts in the East, too. They were not much better off than the West as their government was in shambles. They were able to import from Europe as the Atlantic seaboard was able to dock huge ships with supplies. They still had fuel, electrical lines and communication. Prices of everything were outrageous, and the products scarce. Manufacturing was just beginning to open and find sufficient energy and resources for making all products necessary to sustain people's needs.

Because transportation was still difficult, finding employees and getting them to the workplace limited the size of any operation.

Produce was scarce except for areas that were able to reestablish croplands, find workers, and divert waterways to grow the food crops. California had lost many people, many farms, and the seawater had destroyed fertile farms. So many that survived the catastrophe were starving with so little food and water available. Many cities were still in shambles.

Some communications had been restored. Radio and phones could work if people had electricity.

Fuel was in short supply as most oil had been pumped by electricity. Prices were so high that people were once again grouped in small communities where they could pool their resources. They needed to be able to walk to get what they needed. Community gardens were again necessary. In winter greenhouses had been built to grow and feed the people. Chickens and cows were again common necessities to feed families.

"So now I understand. If immigrants brought money or wealth with them, they could succeed in a new land. If someone came to live with family and their family was established, one could succeed with a bit of time and help. For the rest of refuges, being forced from their homes and their way of life, coming to a new place was-is very difficult," and Beth paused, thinking.

"You start with the clothes on your back. You have skills and knowledge if you are given the chance to use it. You can be driven to work hard, but meeting the expectations of others, following many rules, often unclear, and getting the pay and rewards provided to the natives may not open many avenues for you. It is all an uphill battle!" Beth lamented.

"Well, that may not be the case for people like Anthony with talents and rare skills as a basketball player," said Mac. "He could be a success in short order. For me, an old farmer that has no land, which was my way of life, I am out of luck! I cannot recover the value of that land and the productivity I put into making it work. I do have talents that I might share if anyone needs my input, but these are new crops to me in a new environment. How can I start anew? I figure we owe nothing but have no credit and I question the marketability of my skills!"

John interrupted him. "You are wrong, Pop! You can fix anything mechanical. You can build things with your bare hands. There is a lot of broken equipment, houses, barns, irrigation ditches that need your skills to repair. You are marketable and remarkable!"

Mac rubbed his chin. "Well, I do okay with old technology…"

Mini stood up and looked him in the eye with her hands on her hips. "That is exactly why you are needed now. Farmers cannot get the technology they had. The way forward right now is in taking a step backward and using what is available to grow crops now! Oh, yes, we will renew our Wi-Fi and internet, GPS and automation will return, but we cannot use that now. We need food now! We need our electricity from wind and solar, now! We must change the fuel needed to plow the fields and sow seeds and harvest. Fossil fuels must no longer be the source of our energy. You can create new ideas to change where we have gone wrong in the past." Mini plopped down from her soap box.

"I hope we can," said Marie. "We have been so dependent on satellites being shot into space with rocket fuel made from fossil fuel. Electricity has been created by contaminating our atmosphere using coal or gas or nuclear power. Water generators cannot be the only answer as we continue in drought. Plus why would be want to rerun high line wires to carry power? We already figured out how to drop the need for telephone lines."

John leaned over and hugged his new wife, Mini. "We have something good and valuable to offer these farms here in the north. Using solar is a start but we need to make it more powerful by developing new engines that can convert electricity into heavy duty power. Or maybe develop new devices that replace the need for pulling plows and driving tractors around, altogether!" He was excited by the idea.

Marie responded to his energy. "We have already improved the solar panels and created better storage batteries for the single home. How do we capture the broader spectrum of the sun's rays and safely expand the usage of what God has given us? Our job should not be in trying to control what we have already polluted, but in depleting the damage already done. We may have been given a 'do-over' on what we have messed up so badly."

"Wow, I may have started a brain explosion here," said Beth as she hugged Marie.

Mae brought a cookie sheet from the oven and extended it around the circle to everyone in the group. "Well for me, I am looking at what brings each one of us joy. For me, it is cooking and baking, and caring for my family. I look forward to our family expanding," and she winked at Mini, "and getting to dream and create with grandchildren. I am happy to be part of feeding all of you as you use your creativity and pass it on to new generations."

"So how do we begin?" asked Beth. "Where do we start, or have we already started? The new solar panels collect more energy and have been modified to keep snow off in the winter months. What else might you try to broaden usage to, say, a city or a manufacturing plant. Not everyone can farm. We need clothes and blankets, transportation, self-cleaning appliances, automated dishwashers, hot water heaters, maids, healthcare, airplanes…" and everyone started laughing and throwing out the list of conveniences people had become so dependent upon.

"We know we cannot save the world from our constant need for more. We can do our part in creating new and safer ways to fix what the earth has demonstrated to us that is dangerous and polluting to our children and grandchildren," Beth continued. "I would love to go back to our home and dream it to be the way it was. I know that is foolish, as nothing will be the 'way it was' ever again. Our lives have to be useful in starting new and better ways for our environment, our families and for generations to come."

"I'm with Mae and I want to do what I love to do and what gives me joy. I am going to write about how my 'family'," and Beth winked at Marie, "is using creativity to improve our world and recreate community that works together, prays together, and takes care of each other, as well as all the blessings we have been given. So, if you are going to use your gifts to create new ways and means, I am getting the word out!"